CW00420555

Grayfang Claimed

by Mattie Waters

Copyright © Mattie Waters, 2021

ALL RIGHTS RESERVED. No part of this book may be reproduced in any form or by an electronic or mechanical means, including information storage and retrieval systems, without permission in writing from the publisher, except by a reviewer who may quote brief passages in a review.

DISCLAIMER. This is a work of fiction. Names, characters, places, and incidents either are the product of the author's imagination or are used fictitiously. Any resemblance to actual persons, living or dead, events, or locales is entirely coincidental.

Chapter 1

Jess

As I park behind my father's convertible, I wonder if there's still time for me to make a break for it. I could text my mother and tell her something came up. Maybe a shift opened at the garden center, or I needed more time to study for that big, non-existent Biology exam next week.

But as luck would have it, before I can think of something believable, my parents step out onto the upper balcony, guest in tow. I let out a groan that I can only hope is muffled by my car.

I'm so desperate to leave that, for a brief moment, I wish I was a shifter like my best friend Ellie. But not a wolf shifter. Something more useful, like a chameleon shifter. Then I could blend in with my leather seats, and when my parents looked away, I could make a run for it.

Do chameleon shifters even exist, I wonder?

My mother turns and spots me in the driveway below, then gives me a small, quick wave that says *What are you waiting for? Get in here.*

I sigh, cut the engine, and vow to make this as quick as possible.

My parents and the mysterious guest meet me in the foyer.

"Jessica, there you are!" My mother exclaims, grabbing me and kissing me on the cheek in that awkwardly formal way that I didn't realize wasn't normal until I was in high school. She does a quick double-take at my face, her brows furrowed in confusion, then gingerly tucks a loose lock of hair behind my ear. I know exactly what she's thinking. My hair is a mess, there are bags under my eyes, and my face is probably splotchy without its normal coat of foundation. I'm not at the top of my game.

Well Mother, I think dryly, *I've been falling apart in slow motion for the last month. Forgive me if my makeup isn't done.*

"Have you met David?" she asks.

I shake my head apologetically as the man steps forward. He's tall, with close cropped blonde hair and the fashion that's common amongst everyone from my parent's country club. Even his posture screams Ivy League. "I don't believe I have."

"His father is Dr. Proctor. The one your father golfs with on Saturdays?" I nod politely, vaguely remembering an older man with similar features.

"David just finished up his first semester at Harvard Law." She emphasizes the last part, and then it hits me. This isn't a casual visit.

This is a setup.

I sputter as my mother covertly winks at me then makes up a bogus excuse about helping the cook get the table set for lunch. Then she grabs my father by the hand, dragging him along behind her, leaving me alone with David.

Slowly, I turn to face David and sigh. "She thinks she's sly."

He nods, laughing good-naturedly. "I suppose she does. But most mothers do."

"Good point."

There's an awkward silence as we both stare at each other, unsure of what to say.

"Your mother mentioned that you were going to Harvard Med next fall?" he asks after a moment. "That must be why she wanted to introduce us."

Oh, that's exactly why she wanted to introduce us. There's nothing she'd like more than for me to settle with a good, well-bred Harvard man, but I spare him that detail. "Well, I only just submitted my application last week. I won't know if I've been accepted for another few weeks, probably."

"I'm sure you'll get in." He smiles, and I can see that he's definitely a product of his upbringing. Good manners, easy smile, charming. It's not a bad combination, but it feels… insincere. Stuffy.

Not at all like Troy.

I wince at the thought. Troy shouldn't cross my mind nearly as much as he does. Whatever is going on between us is just a fling. It's just casual sex amongst two people who barely even qualify as friends.

Comparing men to Troy? That's the last thing I need to do, because Troy — or any man like him — is *not* who I'm going to end up with.

I've grown up with the proverbial silver spoon in my mouth. Everything has been easy, and I know it. Since I was young, my parents have thrown their money at whoever and whatever was in my way. Private school, special tutors, exclusive clubs. I've always been grateful for the easy path to success that my parents laid before me. I've always leaned into it.

But a few weeks ago, all that changed.

The world should've felt like it was crumbling around me. Ellie and I took a weekend getaway to the little town of Applecross, deep in the mountains. It should've been a simple, relaxing weekend, but it ended up with Ellie attacked at a bar while I was in the restroom. Next thing I know, there's a mysterious — and handsome — man urging me to follow him. He promised to keep me safe while his brother looked after Ellie, and for some reason, I trusted him.

And so Troy and I holed up in a cheap motel room. It should've been awkward. Instead, it was one of the best weekends of my life. His attention was addictive, his touch mind blowing. At first I was scared and worried, but he made everything okay.

Well, more than okay. Our weekend was exhilarating and romantic and there was a sexual chemistry that I, until that point, believed was only possible in romance novels. Those moments with him made me feel alive in a way I'd never felt before.

And that realization has been a tough pill to swallow, because life feels kind of boring and colorless now.

I blink at David, realizing I've completely tuned him out as I've been lost in thought. I give him a smile as he prattles on about something to do with his law degree.

My mother's matchmaking never bothered me before now. I found it amusing, if anything. But things have changed since meeting Troy. Now, I can't brush off my mother's meddling. In my head, my future husband doesn't look like David anymore. He's starting to look a hell of a lot like Troy.

As my best friend Ellie would say, I've fallen off my rocker.

David clears his throat, pulling me out of my thoughts. "You know, I'm in town for another week. If you want to…"

I know where this conversation is going, and I steer us in another direction. Troy and I aren't a *thing*, but that doesn't mean I'm mentally or emotionally open for dating.

"I need to pee," I blurt.

David's eyes go wide at my bluntness. If I didn't feel like I was on the verge of a mental breakdown, I might find it funny. Instead, I just duck my head and book it down the hall. The bathroom door clicks shut before he even manages out a small, surprised "okay".

I grip the edge of the marble countertop and close my eyes, focusing on taking deep, calming breaths. Not even a month ago, I probably would have been really into David. He's tall, handsome, on a fast track to success. But then I think of Troy. He's a wolf shifter — so barely even in the same world as me — and he's rough and stubborn and definitely not high society with his tattoos and perpetual scowl. But… he's genuine. And he's handsome in that exciting, bad boy way. And he's protective, and…

Damn, I have it bad.

I unlock my phone. My fingers hover over Troy's name, but at the last second, I decide to message Ellie instead.

Are we still on for this weekend? I text. I know the answer already, but just seeing her reply will make me feel better. In this moment, I need a distraction.

Ellie is quick to respond, and if she suspects my motive for texting her, she doesn't let on. *Yeah, girl! Just got back from the grocery store. We're all set for the biggest barbecue of the season!*

I let out a breathy laugh. It's January and there's very likely snow on the ground in the mountains where Ellie lives with her mate, Nathan, and his brothers Troy and Blake. It hasn't been long since she was claimed and bitten by Nathan, but she seems to have adjusted to her new life as a shifter really quickly.

So quickly that she sometimes forgets that regular humans don't have shifter thermoregulation and therefore don't have barbecues in the middle of winter.

Great. I'm so ready. Should I bring anything?

Just yourself, she replies.

Not a second later, she adds, *Nathan says you can bring beer if you want.*

Got it, I reply. I almost ask what beer the boys prefer, but knowing Troy, I suspect that the cheapest beer will do. I'll definitely be making a beer run on the way up there, because

I'm pretty sure the expensive wine and spirits my parents have would be lost on those guys.

I bite my lip as I stare at the screen. Part of me wants to ask about Troy. Has he mentioned me? Am I on his mind as much as he is on mine? It's a bad idea to even ask, I decide. It doesn't matter if he asks about me because it's just a casual fling between us. There's no relationship to be had there. We aren't compatible.

I can't wait, I text. *I need to unwind. Bad.*

I keep the part about my plans to work my frustrations out in bed with Troy to myself.

I'm finally feeling a little better when there's a knock at the door. My mother's voice echoes through the cracks. "Jessica, are you in there?"

I take a deep breath, put on my poker face, then open the door. My mother blinks up at me. "What are you doing in there? Lunch is ready. We're all waiting for you. Is everything okay?"

"Um, yeah. Just a little stomach bug, probably," I lie, clutching my stomach. She winces, nodding sympathetically but struggling to hide her obvious disgust. "Well, don't tell that to David." She grabs me by the forearm, leading me to the dining room. "Isn't he handsome?" she whispers, though the words loudly bounce around the tall, empty hallway. "And he goes to Harvard. Harvard! You two would make a great match. And the babies! With your hair, his eyes… they would be the cutest babies."

I shush her as we approach the dining room. David and my father are already seated at the table, making small talk, probably about something like the country club or golfing or my father's law practice.

My mother flashes me a big, encouraging smile, then leads me to the table and to the spot next to David. He stands as we approach, then pulls the chair out for me.

Suddenly, it's too much. I'm going to scream if I have to

sit in this stuffy room and flirt with boring, clean cut David while my parents sit and watch nearby. I'm actively going through an existential crisis, for heaven's sake.

"I'm sorry everyone, but I really need to get going." I try to keep my voice level and polite, but the disappointment in the room is palpable.

"Where are you going?" Mother asks.

"I'm visiting Ellie this weekend and I need to get a move on if I want to make it before dark."

"Again?" My father asks. "Weren't you just up there a couple weeks ago?"

"Well, she's my friend and I want to see her. And I just feel like I need a break."

Surprisingly, mother nods in agreement, then rubs my back sympathetically. "Oh, dear. That's understandable. I can tell you've been stressed lately."

You don't know the half of it, I think. But still, I'm impressed that she's noticed at all. Even if she'd faint if she knew the entire reason I'm stressed.

"It's probably a good thing that you take some time for yourself, then." David says. "I remember how nervous I was while waiting for my acceptance letter."

"Oh, I'm sure!" My mother enthusiastically agrees.

David smiles up at me. "My parents have a beach house. You're more than welcome to come down and relax there. If you're not busy, we can do next weekend." He pauses, then looks up at my parents. "You can all come. It'll be fun."

"That sounds like a great idea!" My mother says before I can come up with an excuse. "Jessica has always loved the beach."

"Actually, I've really been enjoying the mountains lately," I say quietly.

That stops Mother in her tracks. "But you've *always* loved the beach. You never cared about going to the mountains before. You hated the ski trips we took when you were younger."

It's clear she wants me to elaborate on my sudden shift in preference, but all I can do is swallow hard, feeling my cheeks flush. Sure, there's a reason why the beach doesn't sound as appealing as it once did, but it's not a very PG reason, and one I certainly don't want to talk about in present company.

"Again, I'm sorry. I've really got to go. David, it was nice to meet you," I lie. He flashes that charming, news anchor smile again as I hug my mother and give my father a quick kiss on the cheek.

And as I'm heading out the front door, I can just barely make out my mother's voice. "I sure hope Jessica isn't spending time with those shifters Ellie has fallen in with."

The door clicks shut behind me, and I practically sprint to my car.

Oh, Mother. You have no idea.

Chapter 2

Troy

We manage to clear the patio of most of the snow, and then I get to work on the grill as Blake retrieves some lawn chairs from the shed.

Blake comes back a minute later, and I stare off into the forest behind our cabins as I wait for the grill to heat up and for him to get the lawn chairs set up. I hear him sit down with a grunt, and then we wait some more.

In silence.

As I suspected, this is boring as hell. Awkward, too. Especially when I accidentally look behind me at Blake. We make eye contact, and I physically feel my wolf recoil.

Blake's eyes are wide, his lips in a hard, thin line. He looks just as uncomfortable as I feel. He blinks at me, then motions to the six-pack wedged in the snow beside him.

I nod. Why the hell not? It's not like alcohol will make this situation any worse. He tosses me a beer.

The edge of the grill makes short work of the bottle cap. It falls to the snow as I take a long, refreshing swig and remind myself why I agreed to a barbecue with the pack.

Jess.

Ellie, the alpha's mate, thinks I agreed to it because I'm finally coming around to what she calls "bonding time". But really, it's all Jess. If Jess doesn't show up to this stupid barbecue, then I'm dipping out. Blake can sit out here by himself, silent and awkward while Ellie and Nathan paw at each other. Then, I can retreat back to my den to watch television and try not to think about Jess.

The backdoor of Nathan's cabin slides open. Nathan walks out, down the porch steps, the night's dinner in hand. Ellie prances out after him, clacking a pair of tongs like the world's most excited lobster.

What Blake and I lack in "Grayfang spirit", Ellie makes up for in enthusiasm. She still hasn't realized that, though we're brothers and packmates, we're still wolf shifters. And shifters don't have the same familial bonds that humans do.

Our pack doesn't, at least.

The wolves in us don't much like company. None of us have ever complained about how we don't sit and talk and sing songs around the campfire together. I prefer the solitude of my den.

At least until recently. Now, Nathan's got himself a mate, and she thinks we need to be more friendly. He's willing to bend over backwards to make sure she's happy, and as alpha, he's willing to make Blake and I bend over backwards, too.

My thoughts must be written across my face, because Nathan just gives me a small, apologetic grunt as Ellie hands me the tongs. I nod, take the plate of steaks Nathan holds out, and get to grilling.

There's a fifth steak, I notice. One extra. I try to hide the smile that pulls at my lips.

The others don't need to know how bad I have it for Jess.

Ellie makes a clucking sound, then elbows me in the ribs. Dramatically, she bends over and plucks the abandoned bottle cap out of the snow. "Litter Bug," she accuses.

"Litter *wolf*," I correct.

"So rude," she mumbles under her breath to Nathan as

Blake snickers.

She narrows her eyes at Blake, but continues on, putting on a voice not unlike a teacher trying to wrangle a bunch of Kindergarteners. "This is going to be great!" she says, clapping her hands together. "Steak, grilled zucchini, beer… is there a better meal?"

Her enthusiasm is met with silence. I almost feel bad when her shoulders fall. We're a tough crowd. The food might be good, but it won't carry the conversation.

She's got a noble goal, but you can't force three anti-social wolf shifters to suddenly be best friends. It just doesn't work that way.

At his mate's disappointment, Nathan clears his throat. All eyes go to the alpha.

"Um, since we're all together, I guess now's a good time to share some news."

Ellie beams at her mate. There's love and awe and gratitude in her eyes, and I can't help but imagine what it would be like for Jess to look at me that way.

There's a subtle change in Nathan's posture, a sudden bitterness to his scent that tells me this isn't a happy announcement.

This is something big. Something to worry about. And it's not hard to guess what it is. We're a small pack, hidden away in a small town. The humans here avoid us like we're monsters, and most other packs don't care about us since we're so few in number and so far out in the middle of nowhere.

Our only problem is the other pack across town. And boy, can they be a problem.

"The Smokefur Pack is a mess right now, guys. Just… be careful. Be on the lookout and tell me if you see anything suspicious."

I huff out a breath. "Suspicious? Like what? They've already tried to take our territory and we put them in their place. They tried to steal your mate, and we took care of that too. What else would they be stupid enough to try?"

Blake grunts in agreement, then surprises us all with a rare addition to the conversation. "They're always a mess. They're all crazy."

I raise my beer to that.

"Alex isn't so bad," Ellie adds, her voice quiet. I frown at her. Not because she's wrong, but because I don't want to admit that she's right. Alex, the Smokefur Alpha, is the exception to the rule. The weekend I met Jess, Ellie was taken by a Smokefur as bait, knowing it would instigate a pack war between the Grayfangs and the Smokefurs. Alex prevented an all-out pack war when he sided with us. He killed one of his own so we didn't have to.

If it weren't for Alex, Ellie wouldn't be here. Maybe Nathan wouldn't, either.

So, I guess I'll give him a pass. It's not easy for an alpha to put down one of his own, even if it's the right thing to do. I didn't think it possible, but apparently, there's a Smokefur out there with a conscience.

Nathan rests a hand on Ellie's shoulder, and I try not to get too jealous that my brother gets to be with his mate in these little moments while mine lives fifty miles away and pretends I don't exist most of the time.

"You're right. Alex isn't bad. But… he's not the alpha anymore," Nathan says.

Ellie gasps, and I down the rest of my beer.

Of course. There's always something else.

It's silent as we all process this information.

"What happened?" I finally ask.

Nathan shrugs. "I don't know for sure. I've been keeping in touch with Alex since Ellie joined the pack, but about a week ago, he stopped reaching out. And then when I called again, someone else answered. The new alpha. Derek."

I rack my brain for the memory of a Derek. Vaguely, I

remember a tall guy with red hair and a sandy-colored wolf. "Did Derek challenge him? Or was it…" I glance at Ellie. She's still innocent. New to shifter life. "…Was it a peaceful transition?" That's the least violent wording I can come up with. I'm rude and rough-around-the-edges, but I'm not a jerk. And it's pretty obvious Ellie doesn't need to hear that the guy who once saved her is probably dead.

Nathan shakes his head. "I think Alex is still alive. I just don't know where he is. All I know is that the Smokefurs are going to be even more volatile than normal while their wolves get used to a new pack order."

"And they've shown they can't be trusted," I grumble.

Nathan nods. "Exactly."

The lack of answers frustrates me, but I forget all of it when the sound of a familiar engine hitting the gravel drive hits my ears. Ellie hops to her feet, all excitement, and this time, I feel it, too. It must be obvious, because Blake cocks his head at me in confusion.

I growl as Nathan smirks at me. "Just go with the flow. If it's meant to be, it'll happen."

The urge to throttle him is strong. I don't need advice on winning Jess over.

Okay, maybe I could use a little help, but not from Nathan. It was easy for Nathan and Ellie. They've been up each other's asses since the moment they first met.

But it's not working out the same for me and Jess. Already, we've mated several times, but Jess hasn't given any indication that it's more than sex for her.

I have her body, but I want her mind and spirit, too. And she isn't as ready and willing as Ellie was for Nathan.

Ellie casts me a knowing look over her shoulder as Jess's car appears around the trees, and I wonder if everybody knows my damn business.

My blood goes cold at another possibility. Has Jess told Ellie? Does Ellie know all the explicit details of what goes on in my bedroom when Jess comes to visit? Heat creeps up my neck at the thought.

"Just a tip: don't come on too strong. Jess isn't the type that would like that," Ellie says.

Clearly. I'm not the smartest man, but even I've deduced that by now. The problem is that my wolf doesn't want to "go with the flow" or "give her space". He wants to smother her, cover her with his scent, never let her out of his sight.

Jess climbs out of her car, her pale hair blowing in the wind like she's a damn snow angel or something. Ellie lets out an ear drum shattering squeal, then bounds for her friend as Jess triumphantly holds up another pack of beer.

Their bodies meet with a crash, and then they're jumping up and down, excitedly chattering away like we don't even exist. Nathan chuckles softly, pleased that his mate is enjoying herself. I watch him out of the corner of my eye, confused. My wolf is a jealous bastard. He wants all of Jess's affection. It's mind-boggling that, not only does Nathan not mind that Ellie isn't paying attention to him, but he's happy for her.

I don't get it.

Silently stewing in my frustration, I stab at the steaks on the grill and pretend that I haven't realized Jess has arrived. I motion at the plate next to Blake, and he stands and holds it out while I move the steaks over.

And then I can't help myself. I look over my shoulder at Jess and Ellie.

Jess casts a quick glance in my direction, a small smile on her face like she's pleased to see me, and my heart stops.

I stare back, frozen in place.

That smile makes everything better. Makes standing out here, putting up with my pack, manning this grill, agonizing over whether she cares about me or not? Worth it. I'd do this everyday if she'd just smile at me like that again.

It's a side of her I only suspected was there, but I'd never gotten to see. In bed, she's confident. Takes charge. Challenges me.

I love it, but it's all a game to her. It's just fun.

But that smile, that look… it was different. There was something real there. Something genuine.

Her hold on my heart tightens impossibly more, and then it hits me. I'm not going to be able to keep this up for much longer. Like an addict, I need more.

Blake clears his throat, and I realize I've been staring for too long. Nathan shakes his head and chuckles, like he wasn't in my position just a month ago.

And this time, I only kind of want to punch him.

Chapter 3

Jess

The sun is setting by the time I pull up to the Grayfang cabins. And when I climb out of the car, I barely remember why I'm stressed at all. My problems seem so far away when I'm here.

There's a thick, cozy blanket of snow on the ground. It settles like a peaceful, cozy blanket on the roofs of the three wooden cabins the pack lives in. The smell of meat on the grill wafts through the clearing, making my stomach growl, and I'm cheerily greeted by my best friend.

I love it. There's a quiet peacefulness that I've only ever found here. I can see why Ellie didn't even think twice about leaving her old life behind.

But by the time we've sat down to eat, my affection for the place wanes. It's freaking freezing out here. It's that miserable, throat-burning cold, and yet all the people around me seem unaffected. Happily, they eat and chatter away (well, Ellie does most of the talking), completely oblivious that I'm the only non-shifter and I can no longer feel my toes. I set my plate down and pull my coat a little higher up my neck. I've just got to wait for everyone to finish eating, and then we can all go inside.

Troy looks down at my half-eaten steak, then frowns.

"What's wrong? You didn't like the steak?"

Heat creeps up my neck at his tone. That, and indignation. Sure, Troy is hot. He's got that lumberjack look to him, with his flannel shirt rolled up his strong forearms and the top button undone, showing glimpses of black ink where his tattoos are. But he's also rude. And blunt.

How is he so good in bed?

"It was great," I answer. "I can't eat the whole thing, though."

He looks offended, probably because he did all the grilling. But I don't have a shifter's appetite, and the slab of meat he put on my plate has to be at least thirty ounces.

Nathan perks up from the other side of Ellie. "I'll eat the rest if you don't want it," he says through a mouthful. Before he can finish his sentence, though, Blake leans over, silently stabs my leftovers with his fork, and shovels it onto his plate.

Troy makes a sound of indignant outrage. "Hey, if anybody gets her leftover steak, it's me."

"And why is that?" Ellie asks. There's a sparkle in her eye that says she knows *something* is going on between us, though I haven't filled her in on all the dirty details.

Troy looks over to me for backup, but I just shrug, like I couldn't possibly know why he thinks he's entitled to my leftovers, either.

Blake takes a big, dramatic bite, and then Troy leans over and smacks the plate out of his hands. Blake let's out a low, inhuman growl that makes the hair on my arms stand up, and then they're both standing up, chest to chest, looking pissed.

"Uhh…" I start, because up to this point, I thought this was all a joke. But apparently Troy is very much protective over my food.

Ellie puts her head in her hands and groans. "Come on guys, not again," she says at that same time Nathan says,

"Just don't kill each other."

In the next moment, I'm thrown backward out of my lawn chair. Stunned, I lay on my back, staring up at the night sky. My back aches and my mind is reeling, trying to figure out what just happened. A hand grabs my shoulder, and then I'm yanked to my feet. "Girl, watch out."

It's Ellie. I blink at her. She's stronger than I remember. It's her newfound shifter strength, I guess.

She shakes her head apologetically. "Sorry. This happens every once in a while. I'm trying to work it out of them, but it's difficult."

Nathan moves to stand in front of us, between us and the wolf fight ensuing on the other end of the patio. I'm momentarily annoyed that he's blocked my view with his massive body, but then I hear snarling and growling and my blood runs cold.

Never mind, he can stand there like a shield as long as he wants.

"Should we do something?" I ask. I know there's no *we* in this situation because I'm just a puny human. If I were to intervene, all I'd succeed in doing is getting myself mauled.

But from the wild, angry sounds echoing against the dark forest, I feel like someone needs to do something to stop this. Before someone gets hurt.

Nathan shakes his head. "They'll be done in a minute."

The clang of metal rings through the clearing as someone knocks over the grill, and then I hear the sizzle of the still-hot coals as they burn through the snow.

With a gulp, I peek out from behind Nathan.

Two massive wolves, one brown and one white, bite and snarl at each other. I watch in fascination. I can't pull my eyes away. Not because I'm scared. More like… dazed.

The fight is violent and raw, but there's a gracefulness to their attacks. Pure muscle, these boys are, and though they're scary, I'm in awe of their strength. Their capabilities as shifters. My brain can't reconcile that the two beasts in front of me were two normal-looking men just a minute ago.

And I don't know which wolf is which man. The bigger wolf, pure white except for a patch of gray around his snout, launches forward, plowing into the side of the rusty brown wolf with black patches. The white wolf bites and claws at the brown one's back, drawing an angry snarl from the brown on as he kicks and squirms. I gasp at the brutality, and the white wolf's head snaps to mine.

Immediately, I know that one is Troy. His eyes are a bright, burning blue, larger and more vivid than when he's in his human form, but I still recognize them. The passion and rawness is there, and I'd recognize that anywhere. It's all I've thought about for the last few weeks.

My breath catches in my throat as I stare back at him, taking in his new form. His fur is so white it blends with the snow, and the features on his wide, wild face are so majestic that I can't look away. How can a man so rough also be a wolf so beautiful?

Blake struggles to his feet while Troy is distracted, then bites down hard on Troy's flank.

My heart stops as the snow beneath them turns red. Troy lets out a long, low howl, then collapses into himself. When I blink, he's human again, his howl morphing into an outraged yell.

"You idiot, you bit me in the ass!"

Blake shifts back to his human form, grinning even though he's got a black eye and scratches down his back. Nathan laughs, and even Ellie cracks a smile as Blake gets to his feet, retrieves the now cold and dirty steak from the ground, and takes a big, triumphant bite from it.

But I don't find this amusing at all. My heart races as Troy turns, revealing the severity of his bite wound. I stumble forward before I really think about what I'm doing. "You're bleeding!" I choke out.

Troy turns to me, surprised. His annoyed expression changes to one of surprise. "I'm fine."

"Jess, he'll be okay—" Ellie starts.

"I don't care!" I interrupt. The clearing goes quiet. I don't care, though. "Can you walk?" I ask Troy.

"Yeah," he replies softly.

I swallow hard, then nod as I take his hand and lead him to his cabin. He limps a step behind me but doesn't protest.

I've been in his cabin before, so I open the front door like it's my own and lead him through the living room to the small bathroom at the end of the hall. The light clicks on as we enter, and I direct him to the counter as I dig through the cabinet on the wall for a first aid kit.

It isn't until I find the antiseptic and bandages that I've calmed down enough to take in the damage. But when I finally take in the wound, I find that it's already scabbing over.

"See? It's not that bad. Just a little bite," Troy says softly.

"Mmm," I answer, then get to work cleaning and dressing it anyway. His features are soft as he leans against the counter, patiently letting me tend to the barely-there wound.

To say that I'm embarrassed is an understatement. I made this into a bigger deal than it was. I don't know why. I know he's a shifter, and he heals way faster than a human. And I know he was fighting with his brother. It's not like they either one of them wanted to kill.

But I forgot all that when I saw the fresh wound. When I saw the blood in the snow.

The sight of all the blood, the feeling in my chest as I realized Troy was hurt. I'll always remember it. I shake my head, trying to rid my brain of the image.

"You're going to be a doctor, right?" Troy asks as he watches me thoughtfully.

Despite what just happened, I feel the corners of my mouth twitch upward. He pays attention, then. We've never actually talked about that kind of stuff. We don't talk much at all, really. Our conversations are normally limited to group conversations while we hang out with Ellie and his brothers. Occasionally we'll sneak off for a quickie, but there isn't much talk about the future in those moments.

"Yeah, I guess." My tone is more indifferent than I expected.

Troy cocks his head, confused. "You don't think you can do it?"

"No, I know I can do it, I just…" I pause. Patiently, he waits for me to continue, but I just shake my head. I don't want to talk about it. Nobody knows about the flip-flopping I've been doing in my head over the last few weeks, and Troy isn't the person for me to talk about it with.

I sigh as the familiar, aching feeling of despair fills my middle. There's no escape from my problems, not even in these secluded mountains. Everywhere I go, I'm reminded that there's something not quite right about my life, and I don't know how to fix it. I apply the bandage, then stand up.

Troy turns to face me. We're inches apart, mostly due to the cramped bathroom, but I don't even try to move away.

My frustration must show on my face. "You can tell me anything," he says low.

His eyes are kind, his features soft as he gazes down at me. I love the way he towers over me, the way it feels like his shoulders take up the whole room. And I love his lips, I think as I stare at them.

Slowly, I lean forward, closing the already short distance between us until we're practically sharing the same breath. I reach out and touch my hand to his bare chest. His warmth is comforting.

"I'd rather not talk," I whisper. His body goes rigid as I plant a light, flirty kiss against his lips.

When his eyes open, his pupils are dilated. He watches me intently as I give him a sweet, seductive smile and take his hand, putting it on my waist before kissing him again.

This time it's more urgent. A clear indication of what I want. My tongue swipes over his lips, and he lets out a little groan of pleasure as his lips part, letting me in. Slowly, our tongues dance as his fingers clench and unclench against my shirt.

His hands move lower, drawn to the hem of my shirt and settling against the bare skin of my hip. I lean into him, loving the way his hard length presses against my stomach.

My fingers brush down his front, lower, over his abdominal muscles. I follow the little trail of hair there, taking pleasure in the feel of those delightful muscles twitching as I move over them. He lets out another groan, panting as he watches my face.

I'm so wet already. So ready for this. This is what I've been thinking about all week. This is the distraction I crave.

But when I touch his cock, he grabs my wrist and pulls away.

"No."

Through the fog of my lust, it takes me a moment to realize he wants me to stop. "I need to tell you something," he murmurs.

My heart drops, and I recoil in mortification.

Chapter 4

Troy

Jess flinches like she's been stung at my words.

I was proud of myself. Impressed at the willpower I didn't know I had to stop her — and myself — from going further.

But as she looks at me like that? A combination of hurt, confusion, and disgust? I kind of wish I hadn't said anything.

Her face is bright red as she stares at me. "Well?"

I swallow hard, feeling more unsure of myself than I ever have. I hate it.

But now is the time. There's no turning back now. I've got to tell her.

She blinks at me, waiting not so patiently for me to explain myself, but when I open my mouth, words fail. I'm not good at communicating. Especially when the topic is *feelings.*

"Oh God, is it an STD?" Her eyes go wide and her face drains of color.

I burst into laughter. What an insane guess.

My mate. She's funny.

Her mouth crinkles into a thin line and that adorable crease between her eyebrows appears. The one that only shows up when she's annoyed. This is my mate, I realize.

There's no reason to be nervous about telling her. We're meant to be together. It's fate. She feels the same as me, and it's best just to get it all out in the open.

"You're my mate," I say. The words are sweet, cool relief. I beam at her, then wait.

But as the seconds tick by without a response, I start to worry. She doesn't proclaim her love for me, she doesn't jump into my arms. Her face is blank, like she didn't understand me at all.

To my horror, her expression slowly morphs into devastation. "Oh God, I'm sorry. This is awful. I didn't know —"

I hold a hand up to stop her. "What do you mean?"

This is awful? There's a flicker of annoyance in my chest that I try to ignore, just because I don't want it to ruin this moment. It's got to be a misunderstanding. She just needs to explain herself.

She pushes my hand down, then gives me a look. "Don't interrupt. I'm trying to explain myself. You're mistaken. I'm not your mate."

I close my eyes and take a deep, calming breath. We shouldn't be wasting time talking about this. We should be in each other's arms, enjoying the night. Celebrating the rest of our lives by officially consummating our mating with a bite. If there's anything we need to talk about, it's when she can move in. Or, like, baby names.

"You're wrong." Though I try to hide my impatience with my mate, there's still a biting edge to my words.

She narrows her eyes at me, not nearly as good at hiding her temper as I am. I smile at her, because she's so damn cute. My wolf couldn't have chosen a more adorable mate, even though she's driving me crazy with this nonsense.

"Pretty presumptuous of you to tell me my own thoughts and feelings are wrong," she bites back. "I said I'm sorry. I don't share your feelings."

I refuse to accept that answer. "You wanted me last weekend, and the weekend before, and that first night in the motel when you were screaming my name into your pillow."

Her face goes red again, and I can tell I've struck a nerve. But it's true, and she can't deny it.

"You're so rude. So blunt. Just because you're good in bed doesn't mean I want to date you, or marry you, or be your mate."

I pause, then swallow hard, because her words sting. This night should've been a sweet memory, but it seems like all we're doing is hurting each other with our words.

"I'm blunt, but I'm not mean to you. I'd never be mean to you."

She goes silent, her features softening at my words. Her arms cross under her bust, and all I want is to reach out and touch her for reassurance. But I don't. Not yet.

"You're not mean," she finally concedes, and it's a small weight off my shoulders to know I haven't gravely offended her. "Listen, it's really sweet you feel that way—"

"Sweet?" She's got it wrong. My feelings are tender, sure, but they're expected. Sweet is something you do on purpose. She's my mate. This is instinct. She's mine.

"Don't interrupt. Let me finish." She pauses to see if I'll say something, but I hold my tongue.

She gives me a small, sympathetic smile, then continues. "We're not a good match. You live here, I live in the city. You're a shifter, I'm a human."

"Ellie was all those things, too."

"But I'm not Ellie. I'm Jess, and I'm going to move across country for school, and then I'm going to be a doctor."

There's a shakiness to her voice that tells me she's not so convinced of her own words. I grab her elbows, pulling her close.

"I listened to you. Listen to me, now. You're my mate, and I'm yours. Always. You can deny it, but I feel it. I feel the bond. It's already there." Her eyes dart away under my gaze, and I reach out, gently touching her soft cheek so she looks back at me. "Every morning since the day I met you, I wake up, and you're the first thing I think about. And the last thing I think about when I'm falling asleep. You move here, you be with me, and I'll move this whole damn mountain to make sure you're happy. I'd love you, take care of you, make sure you never wanted for anything. Don't you want that?"

Her eyes are wide, swimming with emotion at my confession. For a moment, I think I've finally gotten through to her. But then she shakes her head. "No. I don't want that," she whispers.

My heart drops. "You don't want that? Or you don't want me?"

"I said I'm sorry."

Desperation turns to anger as I realize she's already made her mind up. "What was the last few weeks for you, then? Just sex? You were just leading me on for fun?"

"It wasn't like that. I thought you just wanted to have fun, too!"

"We're great together," I remind her, one last ditch effort to get her to see reason. "You know that." Even now, as we're fighting, I feel the connection between us. Her body calls to mine. I just need her to realize that.

"That doesn't matter."

"You admit it, then? You want to be with me, but you can't." A chill runs down my spine as I put two and two together. "You don't think I'm good enough for you. I've got too many tattoos, I drive a Harley, I cuss too much. I'm not a doctor and I don't drive a beemer. I don't fit in with your imaginary perfect life, even though you like all that about me."

Jess is completely silent. The challenge, the stubborn fight that's normally in her eyes is gone. And that's how I know I'm right. Only instead of being glad I've won an argument, it just hurts.

My spirit has been beaten down. Defeated.

I turn away, gritting my teeth as I press my palms to the countertop.

The door clicks shut as Jess leaves.

Chapter 5

Jess

When I wake up, my hair is a bird's nest and my eyes are crusty from yesterday's leftover mascara. Mother thought I looked rough yesterday? She wouldn't even recognize me today.

It's impossible to sneak out when you're staying with a bunch of shifters with superhuman hearing, but I try anyway. I'm not at all surprised when I zip up my overnight bag and Ellie pops out from her bedroom down the hall.

She frowns at me, her hair a mess and her eyes puffy from a restful night's sleep. But still, she glows. I guess love does that to you.

Too bad I'm not in love.

"What are you doing? You're not leaving, are you?" There's hurt in her voice, and it makes my heart ache. Of course Ellie would be offended that I'm cutting the weekend so short. But what is the alternative? Stay here to spare her feelings and spend the rest of the weekend avoiding Troy? There's no winning for me. My relationships are falling apart.

Not that Troy and I had a relationship.

Before I can answer, Nathan's head peaks out from the bedroom, too. He takes one look at me, then at my bags, then blurts out, "I thought you'd be with Troy."

I let out a groan. The last thing I wanted to do was explain what happened last night. Not that I wouldn't tell her eventually, but I've barely had any time to process it myself. And, though I've been friends with Ellie since Kindergarten, I know that Troy is part of her pack, now. He's special to her in a brotherly way.

I don't love him, but I'm not a jerk. Bad-mouthing him is not my goal.

And yet, Ellie doesn't look as surprised as I thought she would. "Was it really that obvious?"

"Honestly? Yeah. Troy isn't exactly hiding his feelings. He's normally an anti-social grouch, but around you, he's not."

I cock my eyebrow in disbelief.

"Okay, he tries not to be," she amends.

I plop back down on the couch and sigh. So, he tries to be better for me. Has a man ever been so genuine in his feelings for me? His tone may be rough, but at least he's honest. I believed every word he said, even the sweetest ones about loving me and taking care of me.

And he's hot and sweet and attentive and kind (to me).

The world isn't fair. Why does my future husband have to be a David? How am I supposed to be happy with David when I know men like Troy exist?

Nathan gives Ellie a quick, sweet peck on the forehead, his eyes swimming with utter devotion, before he retreats back into the bedroom. I fight the urge to scowl.

We move into the kitchen, and while Ellie makes coffee, I tell her everything. We slept together the night we first met and it wasn't supposed to be serious. He was just a fun fling to escape the stress and uncertainty I'm feeling in life right now.

It feels good to unload, and like always, Ellie is a great friend and listener.

"It's not my fault he caught feelings. It was supposed to be temporary. He's obviously not my usual type. Maybe I'm going through a quarter-life crisis or something."

Ellie's eyebrows furrow as she takes a long sip of her coffee. A sharp pang of guilt rings through my middle.

"Don't tell me you think *he's* in the right!"

She shrugs, and I can barely contain my shudder of disbelief. That, and jealousy. She's supposed to be *my friend* first. She's supposed to have *my back* before her packmate's. All I wanted was for her to tell me everything is going to be okay. That it wasn't my fault. That the guilt I feel is just me being silly. At yet here she is, confirming that I'm the villain somehow, even if I didn't realize it until too late.

"Jess, it's not how you think," Ellie says at my stunned silence. "I understand where you're coming from. I do. But since I became a shifter…" her voice trails off.

"You're loyal to your pack now instead of me." My voice is bitter. I hate it. Green is not my color.

"Nooooo," Ellie answers. "What I was going to say is that since becoming a shifter, I can relate to them more. As a human, it's hard to comprehend what they feel. The mating thing isn't just like love, Jess. It's on a whole other level. I feel bad for the guy."

"Great, that makes me feel so much better. I *love* that I'm not breaking his heart normally, I'm doing it on a *whole other level*."

Ellie rolls her eyes, but there's a small smile there. "I'm just saying that the mating instinct is probably bigger than you realize. And for what it's worth, Nathan said he's never heard of the mating instinct being wrong. There's always a happily-ever-after." She pauses, then adds, "How cool would it be for you to live right next door?"

I narrow my eyes at her, though I hate to admit, that would be pretty cool.

"You have to admit our lives aren't compatible. He's here,

for one. And I'm moving cross country soon. I'm going to med school. Is he supposed to come visit me at school? He'd stick out like a sore thumb. And he rides a freaking motorcycle. And he's a shifter! You know how my parents feel about shifters."

"I know." Ellie sighs, because she knows all too well. As far as my parents know, she's still a human, only she's gotten wrapped up in the "wrong crowd" and is staying with Nathan. Eventually they'll want to see her again, and they'll find out what actually happened. But neither one of us are eager for that day.

"Then what am I supposed to do? Even if I did like him like that, am I supposed to give up my entire life so that he can be happy?" It was easy for her. She was miserable before Nathan, working a dead-end job as a customer service rep for a bank.

Ellie thinks for a moment, then shrugs. "There's not an easy answer, I guess. But can I say one thing?"

I motion for her to continue, though I brace myself for a verbal lashing about poor Troy and his broken heart.

"The most important thing, at least for me, is that you're happy. I'm loyal to my pack, yes, but that doesn't take away from the fact that we've been like sisters since we were five-freaking-years-old. I love you. And if going to medical school, becoming a big-shot doctor, marrying a successful man and having two kids and a vacation home in the Hamptons is what you want, then I support you."

"Thank you," I whisper, my throat tight with emotion. "That *is* what I want."

With a smile, she pats me on the hand, then gets up for another cup of coffee. And I sit there, silently, wondering why my last sentence sounded like a lie, and why that pang of uncertainty in my middle only grows.

Chapter 6

Troy

I bought my bike because it's fun to ride. Except right now, as three women sit in the car next to me, gawking like I'm famous or something, I wish I was driving something with more doors. And a roof. And tinted windows. Hell, a tank would be nice.

I do my best to keep my eyes up at the red light, but it's damn hard. Without realizing it, I look over. One of the women blushes, then twiddles her fingers at me in a girly wave.

Uhhh, right. I give them a curt nod, then force my eyes back forward. Their giggles are muffled through their glass windows.

And that's why I hate the city. Shifters are a rarity here, and for some reason, human females have it in their head that we're some kind of sex gods. It's weird, though. Not flattering. I feel like a piece of meat on display, riding around on my motorcycle.

Besides, there's only one female I want in my bed, and she's refused to answer my calls or texts for the last month.

How long have I been sitting at this damn stoplight?

A pungent smell hits me like a Mack truck. My eyes water as my head whips to the right, to the sidewalk where a man sits, leaning against the dirty wall of a corner store. His clothes are dusty and worn, his face and hair greasy. His unkempt beard hides his mouth, though I get the feeling he's not smiling, because his eyes are sad as he stares impassively at the sidewalk.

I swallow hard, trying not to breathe through my nose, and I can't look away. The man looks completely beat down, tired and miserable, and yet everyone ignores him like he doesn't exist.

Do humans really have such a weak sense of smell that they don't notice him? No, I decide as I watch people walk by. They walk around him, giving him a wide girth. They're just assholes. I'm rude and kind of scary looking, but I'm not an asshole.

Another reason to hate this city. I jump off my bike, then run over to the sidewalk where the man sits. Quickly, I grab my wallet from my back pocket, flicking it open and throwing a twenty on the ground before I have to inhale again. The man's eyes flicker up to me, like the flame at the end of its wick. "Here," I grit out, just long enough for the man to know I haven't accidentally dropped the cash. And then I run back to my bike, where the light has just changed and the cars in the other lanes are already moving.

"Wait!" the man croaks out before I hit the gas. "Thank you."

I just nod, because I don't want to think about it too much. All I know is that, were this man a shifter, he'd have a pack to catch him when he falls. Few people matter to me, but the ones that do, I know have my back, at least.

The yellow moving truck behind me honks obnoxiously. Patience lost, I turn around and growl at the driver. His face goes pale as he realizes he's picking a fight with someone stronger and wilder than himself.

I floor it through the intersection.

I've got to find Jess, or I'm going to change in the middle

of the city, attack one of these assholes, and find myself with a tranquilizer dart in the ass and a free trip to jail.

It's been years since I've been to the city. I forgot how everything assaults the senses. There's a reason there aren't city shifters. The lights, the sounds, the smells. I feel naked and vulnerable, unable to rely on my senses like usual. And so my plan to scent Jess out isn't going to work, I realize.

I pull into a gas station, then rip my phone from my back pocket. Jess works at a garden center in the afternoons after her classes, that much I know. How many garden centers can there be in this godforsaken city, anyway?

A quick Google search tells me there's far more than I realized. I fight the urge to chuck my phone across the parking lot.

Maybe I should just go back home, chalk this trip up as an unfortunate waste of an afternoon. That would be easiest. But the possibility of facing yet another long, sleepless, miserably lonely night without hearing from Jess sounds unbearable. I do the unthinkable.

Where does Jess work?

I hit send on the text message to Ellie, then imagine her confusion as she gets the notification.

As expected, she ignores my question, guarding her friend's information like treasure. *Why do you want to know?*

Oh, just wanted to pick up some flowers to spiff up the yard, I reply sarcastically. *Maybe some patio furniture so we have somewhere nice to sit during our pack tea party next weekend.*

Are you in the city?

There's that urge to chuck my phone again. *Yes, Ellie. I'm in the city.*

I don't think it's a good idea for you to visit her right now.

My blood boils at the suggestion that I shouldn't see my mate, but I close my eyes and take a deep breath, trying not to pay too much attention to the smell of piss and gasoline and cheap gas station hot dogs.

Jess said I was rude. That that's why she didn't want to be with me. I can't help that I'm a shifter, but maybe I can try to be… a little nicer. Maybe.

Listen, I just want to talk to her. I promise I won't force myself on her, or make her feel uncomfortable, or hurt her in any way. I'd never do that to her. She's my mate. And you're my sister-in-law and packmate now, and I wouldn't hurt you by hurting her, either.

Ellie doesn't respond immediately, and I can guess why. She's probably jumping up and down, excitedly telling Nathan that I'm actually being friendly. That I'm having a "breakthrough".

And I feel like a big, bumbling idiot. I can run faster, bite harder, growl louder than any shifter, but when it comes to my mate, I need help. I have to beg for information from her friend because she wants nothing to do with me.

Carter Seed Company. Good luck, brother-in-law!

She ends the text with ten smiley face emojis, but I'm so grateful that I know where Jess works that I don't even mind.

Actually, I'm damn excited. Within seconds, I've got *Carter Seed Company* in Google, the address, and a mental map of how to get there. My heart's pounding in my ears at the chance to see my mate again after so long.

I start the bike again, but at the last second, decide I need something else. I run inside the convenience store, startling the cashier as I bust through the front doors and frantically search the aisles.

I need something. A gift. Jess deserves that. But what? My eyes land on a bag of beef jerky.

She liked the steak. Surely she'll like beef jerky, then. Everybody likes meat, right?

The cashier flinches as I excitedly slam the beef jerky on the counter with a little too much force.

I pay, then run back outside, hopping on my bike and tucking Jess's gift into my jacket pocket.

It doesn't take me long to find the garden center where Jess works, and I'm only a few blocks away when I catch the faint scent of her in the air.

Today is the day. After a month of no contact, I finally get to see her again. I'll give her the jerky, then apologize for the way I handled our last conversation. I'll explain that she means everything to me, that the last month has nearly killed me, knowing that I might have hurt her feelings and that she probably hates me.

I don't know where to go from there, but right now, with my heart beating at a hundred miles-per-hour and a happy buzz from simply being near her, I'm feeling optimistic. And whatever she decides, at least I got to see her.

I park in front of the garden center, a small shop with vines crawling up the exterior and plants hanging from the windows, tucked in between larger buildings. Following the scent of my mate, I hop off my bike, then head around back, where there's a small courtyard filled with a variety of plants.

And there Jess stands, in the middle of the courtyard, chatting with a customer. In the whole of this Godforsaken city, all gray steel and concrete, she's found the one spot where there's still greenery, still life, still meaning. Amidst the foliage, her yellow hair blowing in the breeze, she looks like a damn wood goddess, and she takes my breath away.

The customer leans forward and brushes her hair off her shoulder, and my heart stops. He talks to her, all cockiness and flirty smile. Blonde, clean-shaven, business suit.

The polar opposite of me.

He holds a bouquet of flowers. With a shy shake of her head, she rejects them as he holds them out to her, and my blood turns to ice.

My skin itches with the threat of an imminent change. That stupid, fragile human male. Cocky because he doesn't know I'm standing here, watching him make a move on my mate.

I'm going to make him bleed.

Chapter 7

Jess

I give the final customer a polite smile and wish her a pleasant evening as she leaves, then do a little happy dance as the door shuts behind her.

My job is great, but so is closing time.

I whistle a little tune as I head outside to check the plants one last time before I head out for the night. I'm straightening up the last few when I hear the jingle of a bell that lets me know another customer has come in. Annoyance bubbles in my chest. I knew I should've locked the door and flipped the open sign to closed.

With a smile plastered on my face, I turn around to see a familiar face.

"David? What brings you here?" I hope that he's not here for me, though I know the possibility is slim. My parents probably put him up to this, told him that I worked here and that I'd be getting off work soon.

Or… maybe he's looking to re-landscape his yard, I think hopefully. But when he makes a beeline in my direction, not even glancing at the plants, I know that was a silly hope. His family probably has a gardener who would handle landscaping, anyway.

"I thought I'd stop by and say hello." His smile is wide,

his posture easy.

I nod politely. "Well, hello."

He doesn't get the hint, or if he does, he ignores it. Instead, with arms outstretched, he leans in, and I'm forced to give him a polite hug.

He pulls away, then presents to me a bouquet of roses. Momentarily, I'm confused, and have half a mind to ask where he picked them up, because I don't see a price tag on them. And then I realize he didn't pick them up from here.

David brought me roses. To my job at a nursery. Where I'm surrounded by a plethora of flowers.

I take them graciously, then sniff at them, doing my best to look delighted. "They're beautiful." It's true, and it's also a kind gesture. But I feel like an ungrateful jerk because I don't fully appreciate them. I can't shake the feeling that it's a generic gift, one he picked because he believes all women love flowers and that's what's expected of him. If he'd have thought even a little bit, I think he would've realized I have access to all the flowers I could possibly want at any time.

It's a generic gift, and it makes me feel like a generic girl. And I don't like that.

I smile at him as he attempts to make small talk, all the while planning in my head a way to cut this visit short while not hurting his feelings.

"So, I was wondering if you'd like to get dinner with me? I've got a reservation for that new Italian restaurant downtown."

"Umm…" Judging by the look on his face, he's all confidence that I'll accept.

"I don't know, I've got to go home and change," I motion to my work apron, worn and smudged with dirt. "Also… I need to study tonight."

His eyes crinkle at the edges, and I wonder if he thinks I'm just playing hard to get. He reaches out, flicking a lock of my hair behind my shoulder, and I shudder at the touch.

Not because he's creepy, but because his touch just feels wrong.

"You work yourself too hard, Jess. Life is meant to be lived."

I shrug, then move behind the register again and dig around in the bins of garden tools underneath, just so I have something to do with my hands. I agree with the sentiment, sure. But I doubt he follows his own advice. He's just playing the role he was taught to play. Be a gentleman, buy the girl flowers, take her out to eat. Then I fulfill my role, where I shyly reject him at first in order to uphold my innocence, though when he counters with an empty platitude, I give in.

Bada-bing, bada-boom, in a year he puts a ring on it, a year after that, a wedding. And then a couple of kids and a boring, unhappy marriage to look forward to until one of us dies.

With David, nothing is genuine. His words are just words. There's no meaning behind them, just like the roses.

I chew on my lip, debating. Maybe I should go. It's clear he's put in some effort. Taken time out of his day to buy me flowers and surprise me at work. And it's not like I've got a reason to say no, really. I don't have a boyfriend.

But honestly? As much as I hate to admit it, I compare every man I meet against a certain wolf shifter. And David can't compete. I'm not interested, and at this point, I'm pretty sure he's not going to grow on me. There's no reason for either of us to waste our time.

I hand the flowers back to him, then shake my head. "I'm sorry. I really can't. You're a great guy, David…" I look into his eyes and see amused disbelief with a splash of overconfidence, and so I decide to go with an excuse I know he can't counter. "I'm seeing someone else."

His brows furrow in confusion. "Your parents didn't mention a boyfriend."

"Um, well, they don't know."

He chuckles, shaking his head slightly. "Well that explains it, then." I exhale a breath of relief that he's apparently not going to keep trying.

Still, he hands the flowers back to me. "Regardless, I bought these for you, so you should have them."

I smile, and this time, I take them gratefully.

The wooden gate at the end of the courtyard slams. Out of the corner of my eye, I see a man rush forward. I let out a yelp as I jump out of the way, just in time for the man to crash into David and pin him to the wall.

I blink and realize it's none other than Troy. His teeth are gritted, his biceps bulging, his eyes a murderous blue as he keeps a struggling David pinned against the wall with his forearm.

"She's *mine.*"

I should say something, but I'm stunned into silence. It's a collision of worlds I didn't think I'd ever see. The man who represents the world I was raised in, and the wild, passionate one that I can't get out of my head.

Slowly, Troy puts more pressure on David's neck. As his face slowly turns purple, I finally recover enough to step in. I lunge at Troy, grabbing him by the arm and pulling him as hard as I can.

He doesn't budge, of course. I'm just a puny human. But I do manage to pull his attention from David to me. "Let him go. You're hurting him."

Troy blinks, and as he stares at me, the churning, violent blue in his eyes fades to their usual icy blue. The muscles of his jaw work, like he's making the hardest decision in his life.

And then he steps back.

David falls to the ground in a sputtering mess, clutching his neck. I step forward to check on him, but Troy lets out a low, feral growl, and I decide it's probably best that I don't.

He looks up at me. "Is this the boyfriend?" he asks, still clutching his neck.

"Yes," Troy growls out at the same time I answer, "no."

David glares up at Troy, still clutching his neck and struggling to catch his breath. He's not dumb enough to fight back, I suppose. "Watch yourself, shifter. If I weren't a nice guy, and if it weren't for Jess, I'd press charges."

Troy growls again, his fists balling up at his side like he's fighting every cell in his body not to attack.

David gets to his feet, and despite Troy standing there, I rush forward, eager to help him up. Like a petulant child, though, he swats my hand away. With a look back at Troy, at his black leather jacket, messy hair, and tattoos, he huffs out a little laugh. "I understand why you didn't tell your parents, now," he mumbles, and I don't know if he realizes how deep he's cutting me with his words. He turns on his feet and storms out without so much as a glance back at us.

I swallow hard. This isn't good. Dread unfurls in my middle as I realize this will inevitably get back to my parents. Probably quickly, too.

I spin on my feet toward Troy, then jab him in the chest. "You come to my workplace and attack a customer? What the hell are you thinking?"

His brows furrow in confusion. He grabs my pointer finger, then gently pushes it down to my side. "I came to visit you."

I could scream in frustration. "You embarrassed me! And you're lucky there weren't any other customers around. Or God forbid if my boss had seen. I'd be fired!" I'm shaking with anger, the edges of my vision red. I haven't been so angry in a long time. Maybe ever.

Gritting my teeth, I stomp over to the register again, clumsily jerking at the tie of my apron. It's doesn't cooperate. I growl out something pitiful compared to the blood-curdling noises Troy made a minute ago, then give up and just angrily rip it off over my head. When I turn around to place it on the hook, Troy is right behind me, not even six inches away.

Silently, he looks down at me, and I want to scream in his face. But instead, I just stare back, breathing heavily, studying his features.

He shoves a plastic bag at me. Confusion trumps anger. I grab it and peek inside and...

Laugh. Out of all the things I imagined in this bag, it wasn't beef jerky. I hold it up to him, then laugh harder. He sucks in a breath, looking the definition of flustered. "What's so funny?"

"What is this?"

"It's a gift."

I take a deep breath, willing myself to calm down. "And why did you bring me a gift?" I ask, wiping the moisture from my eyes with the back of my hand.

"I wanted to apologize. I wanted to talk to you." His features go soft.

That sobers me up. My heart melts at his admission. "I kind of want to talk, too, I guess," I answer quietly.

For the last month, I've ignored his attempts to reach out, but I still feel bad about how our last conversation went. Over and over, I replay it in my head, and the more I try not to think about it, the more space it takes up in my brain. I just want to move on with my life. And maybe to do that, we need to talk.

Without thinking, I smile. And it's genuine. Effortless. His hand is warm and comforting when I reach out, grabbing it and pulling him toward the door.

I missed his touch, I realize.

"Let's go talk, then."

Chapter 8

Troy

Jess laughed in the face at my gift, but now she eats it as she paces in front of me, making soft, appreciative noises like she's eating the tastiest ribeye. My mate is a confusing one.

I watch her in fascination, the wolf in me taking pride in providing food for her. Her eyes flutter open as if she's just remembered I'm here, and her face flushes. "Sorry, I was hungry." She apologizes, then holds the bag out to me. "It's really good. Try some."

I take a piece from the bag, making sure I brush my fingers against hers because I can't help myself. Shyly, she averts her gaze to the floor, then grabs another piece of jerky and pops it in her mouth.

We eat in silence, and all I want to do is say, "See? I told you I'd take care of you!" But I don't. I sit quietly, right at the edge of her bed, determined to keep my mouth shut like my life depends on it.

Because if there's one thing I've realized when it comes to my mate, it's that things don't go wrong when I'm quiet.

Jess opens her mouth like she wants to say something and I brace myself for *the talk*. But she snaps her mouth closed again, then shakes her head. "I need something to wash it down, I think." She stands, then crosses the room.

Hesitantly, she glances back at me. "Would you like something to drink?"

I think for a moment, then nod my head. "Beer would be nice." Hopefully four words isn't enough to ruin everything.

She grins as she shakes her head. "I don't know if I'll be able to find any of that. My parents aren't really beer drinkers. But I'll try to find a suitable substitute."

I nod my head as she disappears down the hallway.

Of course they don't have beer, I think, feeling like an idiot. *Can you not pretend to be fancy for one night?*

My hands are cold and clammy. I opt to wipe them on my jeans instead of her expensive looking blanket. I'm both nervous and eager for Jess to return. Nervous about what she's going to say, nervous about what I'll say to fuck things up even more. The last thing I want to do is push her away. I don't know if I can go another month or longer without seeing or talking to her.

From my post on her bed, I glance around Jess's room. It's... not what I expected. The room is probably as big as my entire cabin, the furniture triple the cost. Tall ceilings with elaborate molding, fancy wallpaper, thick, heavy furniture. I'm no interior designer, but even my uncultured eye can see that everything is carefully curated, everything is expensive, and everything has a place. I sit up a little straighter, suddenly feeling a bit underdressed, though Jess and I are the only two people in the house.

But now I understand what she meant the last night we saw each other. About me, a shifter, not fitting into her life. And then I think of that dickhead David at the garden center and how he said, in that fancy, disgusting accent of his, that he could see why Jess never told her parents about me.

I was angry then, but now I just feel like dirt. I can't be angry with something that's true.

Now I understand that defeated, beat down look in the homeless man's eyes. That's the look a man has when he's convinced, deep down, that he's not good enough.

That's what it all comes down to. I'm not good enough for Jess. Story of my life, I guess. I wasn't enough when my parents and my brother needed me most, and now my parents are dead and my brother scarred.

Back then? I was not old enough, not strong enough, not brave enough.

Same old story now. Not enough then, not enough now. Not rich enough, not successful enough, not human enough.

And I'm probably going to lose Jess, just like I lost my family.

I'm staring at the fluffy white bedding, lost in thought, when Jess returns. She thrusts a glass of something foul into my hands. I stare at it in the glass. It's a deep amber color, harmless looking, but it makes my eyes water at the same time.

Jess giggles, then clinks her own glass against mine and takes a gulp. I follow suit, deciding if she's brave enough to try this poison, I suppose I am, too.

It tastes like a mixture of kerosene and bear piss, but I try my hardest not to cough and sputter. Jess hisses as she swallows it, then blinks back tears. "Oh God, that's awful."

I bark out a laugh, relieved that I don't have to pretend to like it, too. "Why would anyone force themselves to drink this?"

She smiles at me, then lifts her glass, studying the poison from the side. "It might not be good, but it's expensive. That's enough to fool my father into drinking it."

At the mention of her parents, my mood sours again. Jess sits down next to me, chattering away about how her parents are out of town, her lips loosened from whatever the hell that drink was. I listen politely, but it's hard to concentrate with the knowledge that, eventually, the conversation will turn and Jess will probably shatter my heart with a sympathetic smile.

Jess stops mid-sentence. "Are you okay?" she asks.

No, I want to say. *My mate will never be mine.*

If the man in me was stronger, if I weren't ruled by an asshole dominant wolf, then I'd leave. I'd give up, resign myself to a lonely, soulless life in my little cabin in the mountains. I'd get up and leave, spare myself the heartbreak of hearing Jess say everything out loud.

But the wolf inside me won't give up so easily. I'm not good enough to be her mate, but there's one thing I know.

No one else can give her pleasure like I do. No one else can tame her in bed. Her body calls for no one's but mine.

My eyes go to her lips. She bites on her lower lip, a nervous habit of hers, I've learned, and there's an expression of deep worry on her face.

My poor, worried little mate.

She insists that we aren't meant to be together. That she doesn't want me in that way. That I'm confused, that the chemistry between us is nothing but hormones.

Even if she refuses to be with me, I'm going to prove to her that there's no one else that can please her like me.

Jess lets out a squeak of surprise when my hand wraps in her hair and I pull her close. I stare into her eyes, not an inch in front of me, daring her to tell me to stop.

But she doesn't, as I knew she wouldn't. Our relationship is an unlit match in a pool of gasoline. We can stay away from each other, pretend all this is nothing, but once that match is lit, we're hopeless to stop it.

She licks her lips and whimpers. Such a princess, my mate is. She's always gotten what she wants. And now she wants a kiss, and I'm not going to deny her.

I jerk her head the rest of the way to me, not rough enough to hurt her, but hard enough to remind her that I'm the shifter here and I'm in charge. Her hands grasp at my shoulders for support as she climbs into my lap, moaning as our lips work over each other.

Her tongue runs over the seam of my mouth and I open, letting her in. She's enthusiastic, even after going no contact for so long. It fills me with dark pleasure, knowing that we can be apart and no matter what, when we come back together, the fire still burns.

Hungrily, desperately, I tear at her jeans. She lets out a hiss as I roughly jerk them down over her supple hips, then tear at her panties. I don't care if I'm moving fast. I want her *now.*

My fingers go straight for the prize. Jess's grip on my shoulders tightens and she sucks in a breath as I run my middle finger through her slit. She's already wet, but I need her dripping for me.

She casts me a look of uncertainty as I add another finger, dipping it into her well. I growl a warning. I know exactly what she's thinking. She's replaying our last conversation, she's worried about my feelings, she feels guilty for leading me on.

Two fingers in, and I palm her clit. She lets out a cry of pleasure as I work in and out of her, deeper and harder with each thrust. But still, her brows are furrowed and she opens her mouth like she wants to insist I stop.

The flicker of irritation turns into a spark of sudden, hot anger. Abruptly, I pull away. Jess makes a panicked, desperate sound in her throat, her face flushed and the scent of her arousal hanging thick in the air.

I flash her an evil smile, enjoying the way she pants, the way her eyes are reeling from the denied orgasm.

Oh, but she's my mate, and if she wants a release, she'll get it. I'm just tired of being on the chasing end. Of being the one pining after her, being the one that cares more.

"Do you want it?"

Jess nods frantically, then reaches for my belt. I push her hand away. "Then say it. Tell me you want my touch. Admit that we have something special."

Her face is utter confliction. She stays silent.

My heart pounds in my chest. I can feel my wolf working his way out. My dick is hard as a rock in my pants, but still, when Jess reaches, I somehow find the willpower to push her away.

"Say. It." I grit out.

"Troy—"

"Fine, then admit that when I walk away after tonight, you'll never think about me again. That you'll move on and find someone else." If she really doesn't have feelings for me, then she should be able to say those words, no problem.

More of that dark pleasure fills my chest as her eyes burn with devastation. She opens her mouth, but the words don't come out.

And that's all I need to know.

I grab her hips, then toss her onto the bed, renewed in my goal to pleasure her so hard tonight that she can't think straight tomorrow morning. I'm going to make my mark on her, just like she's made her mark on me.

And I'm going to enjoy every second of it.

Wordlessly, we scramble to remove our clothes, and then she's naked, sprawled out before me, her chest heaving and her pussy slick with need.

I take a moment to savor the sight, then shake my head. "Face down, ass up, princess."

She crawls to her knees, then arches her back, presenting herself to me. My mouth waters with the urge to taste her, but it's not about me right now.

I slick my finger through her folds, soaking in the sight of her flushed skin. She blubbers nonsense into the bed covers, grasping wads of it in her fists like those covers are the only thing keeping her from flying away.

I dip into her well once more, and when I feel her muscles contract around my fingers, her body rocking against my hand, desperate for a release, I pull away again.

She cries out in frustration. "Please, Troy! I need to come!"

I smile, but don't immediately answer. All the times we've mated before, it's never been like this. Then, the sex was light, playful. She was all smiles and giggles. It was all about having fun.

Now, there's a desperate edge to us both. There's hunger and need in her eyes as she pouts at me over her shoulder.

"Please," she says again. "I need you."

I allow myself a second to savor those words before I mount her. I know what she really means — that she's so close to climax that she wants me to go on and finish the job. But I give in to the little ball of hope in my chest and let myself, for at least tonight, believe she wants more than she actually wants.

Like me.

Her patience runs out, apparently, because her hands move to her pussy. Gently, I bat her hand away, then grab her hips and direct her onto her back. My cock is practically throbbing as I position myself at her entrance.

I suck in a breath as I enter her, the sensation of her warm, wet core and all the teasing making me already close. Her legs wrap around my waist and then she pulls me deeper into her. I growl, then wad her hair through my fingers, pinning her beneath me.

Maybe I'm a little rough. I pound into her hard and fast, instinct taking over and my restraint melting away at the feel over her muscles clenching around my cock. She's a loud one, my mate. With eyes squeezed shut, her beautiful lashes brushing the tops of her cheekbones, her blonde hair a knotted mess around my hand and on the pillows, she screams out her pleasure.

Those noises drive me harder, faster.

Impossibly, I crave more of her. More scent, more touch. I lean forward, chest to chest, and bury my nose in her neck. She digs her fingernails into my shoulders, her heels into my back, pinning me in place just as much as I pin her. I pump into her, feeling my release close.

In this moment, we're as joined as two people can be. Except...

I feel my fangs extend. I could bite her, and then she'd be mine forever, whether she wants it or not. Never have I felt a stronger temptation as when I open my mouth, scraping my teeth over the delicate skin of her neck. I lick at her skin there, then nip at it gently. Not enough to break the skin, not enough to change her, but enough for her to realize my intentions.

She gasps in delight as my teeth tease an unspoken promise. "You could be mine," I grit out. "All I'd have to do is bite."

And then she explodes.

I growl out something monstrous as my own release hits me like a freight train. Over and over I pound into her, emptying my seed into her, claiming her hard and thorough.

Jess lays still underneath me, breathing hard, utterly exhausted. I feel the same. Hesitantly, because I don't want this moment to end and us to go back to the way we were, I roll off the bed.

I dare just a peak at Jess before I get dressed. Her eyes are closed, a slight, sleepy smile on her face. She's sprawled, just as I left her, her legs still spread and her head tilted to the side, neck exposed.

There's a fierce surge of pride as I take in her used, exhausted body. Because she's recovering from *me*. That smile of satisfaction? From *me*.

At the zip of my jeans, Jess cracks open an eye and frowns at me. She sits up, then reaches out a gentle hand on my forearm. There's an unexpected sadness in her voice as she says, "Will you stay the night?"

My heart squeezes. Sleeping beside my mate will only make me fall deeper. I don't think I can stay here tonight, cuddling with Jess and soaking up her limited love, and then

leave tomorrow a whole man. She'll break me.
    And yet I nod, because I can't say no.

Chapter 9

Jess

When I roll over, my hand automatically reaches out, searching for Troy. My heart squeezes as my fingers brush his warm back.

He was right. There's no one that makes my heart beat like he does. There's no one else that induces a pit of dread when I first wake up and worry that he's not next to me.

There's something special about the man lying next to me. I never thought I was the submissive type in bed, but after last night? My toes curl of their own accord when I think about how thoroughly he claimed me.

When it comes to Troy, I'm okay with being submissive. I trust him. I know he'd never hurt me, never break my trust by abusing his strength.

Everything feels natural with him. And so freaking delicious. I prop my head up in my hands and watch him sleep. His face is relaxed, his mouth slightly parted as he snores softly. The lines of his face, normally twisted in a scowl or giving someone the stink eye, are smooth in his restful sleep. Like this, he's got a boyish attractiveness about him.

Part of me wants to wake him up with a blowjob, but a larger part of me wants him to sleep.

Let him get a few more hours of peace, because when he wakes up…

My heart squeezes. We got so distracted last night that we never actually talked.

Quietly, I shuffle out of bed, trying not to think about how not even twelve hours ago I was so sure that, if I could just explain to him why we weren't good together, everything would be fine.

Why is it so easy to convince myself that I'm okay without him when there's distance between us? But then, the second he shows up in town, all that goes out the window? Why does our relationship feel like a ticking bomb? Like, as long as we're far enough apart, as long as I try to pretend I don't want him, everybody is safe. But when we're close, we're in the danger zone?

I pad into the kitchen, make myself a cup of espresso, and sit down with my laptop at the kitchen bar. It's habit now to check the status of my med school application as soon as I open my laptop.

But like every other morning for the last month, it says the same thing. *Pending Review*.

I let out a sigh. The uncertainty is the worst part. Everything hangs onto this one decision that some old fart at Harvard is taking his sweet time to make. If I could just find out one way or the other, then I could move on. Start making plans. Start taking the next steps.

The cursor hovers over the words. I stare at them intently, like I can magically will them to change before my eyes. I'm only extremely confused and disturbed when I realize I'm imagining the status changing to *rejected*.

Something touches my shoulder, and I nearly fall out of my chair. Troy laughs softly, an apologetic look in his eye. "Sorry," he says sheepishly.

I feel my cheeks turn scarlet. I don't know why. It just feels like things are different between us after last night.

More complex.

Not that our relationship was all that tidy to begin with.

"It's okay," I say, nervously smoothing my pajamas. "You're up earlier than I thought you'd be."

He shrugs. "I can go back to bed if you like."

There's still that raw edge to him, that bluntness that is so Troy. But his voice is soft, his features kind. His eyes crinkle in amusement.

Butterflies flutter about in my stomach. Mentally, I shoo them away. After we talk, they'll all drop dead, anyway.

"Want some coffee?" I ask. I tell myself that it's the polite thing to do, when really, I just trying to delay the inevitable.

I fumble about the kitchen, hyperaware of my movements as he watches me. I suddenly wish that I'd thought to get dressed or brushed my hair or *something* before he came downstairs.

Things were simpler when I didn't care. When I thought we were just using each other for a fun bit of stress relief on the weekends.

"You're cute in the mornings, you know that?" He says, smiling gratefully as I hand him a cup, then takes a sip and sputters. "What is this?"

"A latte?"

I grimaces. "I... don't think I like it."

He looks utterly mystified, and I can't help but laugh at his expression. Nothing has gone right since we arrived here last night. First, I serve top-shelf whiskey and he nearly chokes, and now I serve fancy artisan dark roast coffee and he thinks it's equally awful.

Troy in my parent's house is like trying to shove a round peg in a square hole. I sigh, realizing that there's no use in putting it off any longer.

I sit down in the chair next to him, then tilt my laptop screen so he can see it. He looks at it with interest, then lets out a low whistle.

"I knew you were smart, but I didn't realize you were *Harvard* smart."

I feel myself blushing again. I know he means it as a compliment, but it makes me uncomfortable for some reason. "It's not a big deal, really. And I haven't even been accepted yet."

He bumps his shoulder into mine, and those stupid butterflies take flight again. "Hey, don't try to downplay it. It's a huge accomplishment. And I'm sure you'll get in." All the sincerity in the world is in his voice, but I swear I also hear a little disappointment.

"I've never said this aloud to anyone," I start. He cocks his head, intrigued, but doesn't interrupt. "I'm starting to second-guess myself."

"How so?"

I swallow to compose myself, but when I speak, my voice is still shaky anyway. "I don't know if this is what I want anymore. I'm not sure Harvard is for me."

His eyebrows furrow, but there's a spark of something in his eyes. Hope? "Ellie said you've wanted this since you were a little girl?"

I make a sound of annoyance. "How much did Ellie tell you?"

"Not much. She's a good friend. Refused to give me any information."

I smile at that. Because not only has Ellie been a good friend and kept my secrets, but now I know that Troy has been asking about me.

"Well, she's right. All this," I say, motioning at my computer, "has been my life plan since before I could walk, probably. Everyone in my family — my parents, my grandparents, my cousins — all went to Harvard in some capacity. I've had private tutoring lessons since I was 10, preparing me for the SAT, getting me ahead of my peers so I have an edge on the application. It's everything I've ever wanted."

"Then why do you not sound convinced?"

I stop, stunned. He just called me out. No one before him has guessed it until now, and here he is, guessing what I'm going to say before I've really even processed it myself.

We stare at each other. "You," I finally say.

His eyes flash, his nostrils flare, and he nods jerkily.

"I like you a lot, Troy. You're the reason I'm second guessing everything."

I hold my breath, waiting for him to say something. I don't know what I expect from him. I've already told him that we can't be together, that there's no way for our lives to mesh together cleanly.

"I don't want to be the reason you abandon all your dreams," he finally says.

"What if I'm not sure if going to Harvard and being a doctor really is my dream? What if I just thought it was because that's what I've been told since before I could have form thoughts of my own?"

He shrugs, then looks down at his coffee, a poor but cute attempt to hide the spark of hope in his eyes. It should annoy me, but I find that all it does it endear him to me even more. He wants me to choose him, sure, but I also believe he wants my happiness. "All I can say is that you should follow your gut, Jess."

"What if I don't know what it's telling me? What if I don't know what makes me happy?" It comes out as barely more than a whisper. Just a breath, really, but the words hang heavy in the air between us.

He stands and pulls me out of the chair. Tenderly, like I'm something fragile and precious, he strokes my jaw, then leans down and presses his lips against mine.

I should protest. This conversation was supposed to be me breaking up with him for good. And yet, as his lips move, mine move too. It's like he's reminding me that, though this isn't a fairy tale, the passion and chemistry between us is something magical.

And more and more I want this magic, not the unfeeling, clinical dream in my head, the weird anti-chemistry of a marriage of convenience and appearance with someone like David.

I want everything Troy has to give. I want to throw caution to the wind, to jump in his arms and see where life takes me. I want to do what makes me happy.

His tongue slicks against my mouth, and I open for him, loving the way he tastes, even with his coffee morning breath. Our bodies melt into each other. With a flick of his tongue, he teases me into opening my mouth wider. Over and over his tongue slicks against mine, invading my mouth, reminding me of last night. I moan and squeeze my legs tighter together, needing more friction, more pressure on my most sensitive spot. I clutch at his arms, desperate for more.

My head spins as he pulls away, and I vaguely remember that we were talking about something. That I had something important I needed to tell him.

The sad look in his eyes pulls me back to Earth, and with a sick feeling in my stomach, I remember. He looks at me expectantly, like he already knows what I'm going to say. I find myself wanting nothing more than to tell him what he wants to hear. I hate seeing that pain in his eyes, especially because I know I'm the one that caused it.

"We don't have to say goodbye completely," I say. "You can come visit me in Massachusetts, and I can visit you when I come home for the holidays."

Troy scowls at the suggestion, and my heart sinks further. He shakes his head. "As much as it hurts, I understand why you're making the choice you are. But this mating thing isn't something you can half-ass. I can't be your secret. I can't be the other man when you inevitably find someone else. I need all of you." He presses his forehead to mine, then closes his eyes and takes a deep breath.

My throat feels tight. I want to insist that he would never be the "other man", that he'd always be number one, but I don't trust my voice at the moment.

He kisses me one last time, a quick, chaste peck that feels wrong coming from the man with so much passion it's like wildfire. And then he turns on his heels and leaves.

I stand alone and confused in the kitchen, frozen in place by shock. The front door clicks closed and a minute later, I hear the rev of Troy's motorcycle, and then the sound of the engine fading away.

My feet feel glued to the floor, my mind slow and heavy as I try to process what just happened.

That was goodbye. Forever.

Ungracefully, I fall back into my chair.

I think Troy just broke up with me.

Chapter 10

Troy

"You just going to sit there like a log for the rest of time?" Nathan asks from behind me.

I growl a non-answer. Maybe I will. There's nothing better to do. Nothing to look forward to.

"You're depressed," Nathan mumbles as he takes a seat next to me, the lawn chair groaning under his weight. He frowns down at the plastic under his ass. "I don't think Ellie took into account how heavy we are when she ordered these."

I shrug, uninterested in his attempt at conversation. I've been pretty uninterested in everything since I left Ellie's house a week ago. About all I've done is sit alone in my den, drowning in my thoughts. And when it gets too bad, when it feels like my wolf will force a change and go find Jess himself, I come outside and sit around the fire pit.

It must really be over, because she hasn't contacted me. We did this before, and I didn't think it possible, but it hurts even more now. There's a real finality to it this time.

Maybe I'm not enough for her. Okay. But hell, I thought we could work through that. I thought that she'd grow to love me as I am. I think she did, in a way, but it wasn't enough.

Because in her eyes, there's one part of me that's unfixable. I'm not a half-ass kind of guy. I want all of Jess, not just the quiet, private parts she keeps hidden from public eye. I want us to belong to each other fully, body and soul, and I want the entire world to know it. My wolf won't allow anything less.

And Jess isn't capable of that.

"Get out of your thoughts," Nathan says, nudging me in the arm.

I scowl, but my growl dies in my throat. Nathan casts me a look of pity, and wouldn't you know it, I finally feel something other than misery and despair.

…Annoyance.

"I'm fine. And I don't need you out here trying to cheer me up. You can go tell your mate that you did your duty and tried to be nice."

Silently, he stands, then makes his way back toward his cabin. I breathe a sigh of relief, sinking back into my chair, until I hear his footsteps crunching through the snow again. He returns with a few pieces of firewood that he chucks into the fire pit and a few pieces of dryer lint for kindling, then produces a lighter from his pocket. One flick later, he's got a fire going, and I guess he's planning on sticking around for a while.

"What are you doing?" I grit out, not even trying to hide the rough edge to my voice anymore. Any patience I had burned away as Nathan started that damn fire.

"Ellie didn't send me out here. I came out here because I wanted to." He stands, hands on his hips, his eyes on the woods. I squint at him suspiciously.

More footsteps crunch through the snow, and Blake appears out of nowhere. I throw my hands in the air. "Is there a party I didn't know about?"

Nathan snickers, but Blake just flashes me a sly grin, then produces a can of beer from his coat pocket. He holds it out to me like he's some kind of beer fairy.

"Fine, you can stay," I grumble.

He's got two more beers on his person, and soon, we're all sitting around the fire, drinking in silence.

Except… it's not that bad, I realize. A couple months ago, when it was just us guys, we never did this. We never voluntarily spent time together. We were of the same pack, but really, we were just a loose grouping of lone wolves.

And now we're hanging out like… brothers. Weird. Maybe Ellie's plan to force us to bond is actually working.

And as much as I hate to admit it, I do feel a little better with them around. The biggest part of me is still a few hours away in the city, but with Nathan and Blake around, I feel a little less broken.

Still pretty fucking broken, though.

I down the last of the beer, then crush the can in my hands and let it fall to the ground. Without a word, Blake produces another beer, and I kind of want to ask where he's keeping them, but he probably wouldn't answer me anyway. And also, I don't care. He's the beer keeper around here. He's allowed to have his secrets.

I pop the tab and take a swig, letting the smooth, malty liquid run down my throat like medicine. With a nod, I study the can.

"She tried to poison me."

Blake and Nathan both look at me, Nathan cocking his eyebrow. "It was some kind of fancy scotch, I think. Tasted awful."

"She's got expensive taste," Nathan says, grinning.

I shrug, not entirely sure that I agree. She drives a car worth more than my cabin, wears nice clothes, drinks fancy wine. But I never thought that's really who she was. It's just how she was raised.

I shake my head of the thought. That kind of thinking isn't useful. All it does is give me hope. What I *should* be telling myself is that she *is* just as snobby as she seems. If I could convince myself of that, maybe I could finally get it through my thick skull that it's never going to happen between us.

"Too expensive for me," I finally say with a scowl.

"If that were true, she wouldn't be your mate."

I ignore Nathan's words, grit my teeth and stare at the fire some more while regretting saying anything at all. Hanging around the fire with my brothers wasn't all that bad when we were sitting in silence. Now, I have half a mind to throw some snow on the fire and stomp back to the solitude of my cabin.

"When is the last time you tried to contact her?" Nathan asks.

That's the final straw. He's well-meaning with his encouragement, but all it's doing is poking at the wolf inside, instigating a fight.

"Listen, I don't mind if you two keep me company, but there's a rule. And that rule is that you sit back and shut up while I complain." My grip on my beer tightens as I take a deep breath, trying to control my temper. "Don't fucking try to cheer me up. Don't try to convince me there's hope. Because that's not what I need right now."

Nathan narrows his eyes at my tone, and I stand up, ready to pick a fight. I don't care that he's the alpha. I'm not as dominant, but my wolf will sure as hell hold my ground on something like this.

But Nathan doesn't shift, doesn't move to fight. Confusion sets in as his mouth twitches, pulling his scars down into a frown. "I'm not going to let one of my pack — my own brother — live a miserable half-life because he's too damn stubborn to fight for what's his."

He blinks at me, waiting for a response. My eyes run over his scars again.

Something inside me cracks. A flood of memories of that

night fifteen years ago, when we nearly lost everything.

Despite trying my hardest never to think about it, I still remember all the sordid details like they're projected on a high definition TV right in my face.

The eerie howls of unfamiliar wolves woke me out of a deep sleep. Goosebumps popped up on my arms as I immediately knew something was wrong, even if I didn't understand what was going on.

I kicked out from underneath my blankets and ran out into the hallway. At the same time, a scarless, anxious Nathan peaked out of his room. A second later, Mom burst down the hallway, clutching a small, crying Blake.

She shoved Blake into Nathan's arms, then looked us both in the eye as she pleaded for us to watch him. Stay inside, no matter what, she insisted before she ran toward the open front door, toward the sound of the most vicious wolf fight I'd ever heard.

I could barely hear my own voice over the howls outside. To my side, Nathan stood wide eyed, as if frozen in place. In my eyes, he'd always been my infallible older brother. He always knew what to do. Now, his fear only made the situation seem even scarier.

A tortured scream rang through the night, then utter silence. Even my wolf, barely more than a pup, only having just experienced my first shift, understood what just happened. A shadow passed the window, and I knew in my heart that it wasn't Mama or Dad. Nathan gulped, then shoved Troy in my arms before crouching low.

I knew he was going to shift. "Mama said to stay inside!" I whispered.

The shadows outside stilled.

"You stay inside." There was something in his voice, something more man than boy, more wolf than man. Something that Dad had that made us listen, made us listen when Mama had had enough.

The moment I realized what that meant must've shown on my face. "Stay here," Nathan, my older brother, my hero, and now my alpha, hissed again, but there was more sympathy in his voice this time, more pleading. And then he shifted and ran out the door before I could even nod.

Blake clung to my neck and I patted his back, unsure of what to do, even as the sounds of another wolf fight broke out.

Nathan was on his own. We were on our own. And though I knew my brother was strong, knew he was brave, I didn't know if he could take on the shifters that had just taken our parents from us.

As quiet as I could, mindful of what little scent the wolf in me gave off, I padded, terrified, to the window and looked outside.

My stomach turned at the sight. Two massive wolf shifters, blood thirst in their eyes. My brother, smaller than both, fighting for his — for our — lives.

Blake whimpered, and the head of the wolf closest snapped to the window.

Nathan saw the opportunity, and immediately jumped on the larger shifter's back, not thinking about the second shifter behind him.

Instinctually, I knew it was the end. Father had drilled it in us from a young age. Never, ever give your back to the enemy.

My shift wasn't a conscious decision. I barely even knew how to shift, really, being so young. But I knew that Nathan, though he sunk his teeth into the neck of the closest wolf, had no hope of surviving the second wolf who stalked closer. And so, without regard for my own life, without realizing that I was making it worse, I dropped Blake and shifted, running out the door.

The look of utter terror in Nathan's eyes as I bounded out the door didn't stop me. The last remaining wolf attacked, landing hard on Nathan, and the sickening crack of broken bones echoed through the night air. Claw and fang ripped into my brother, my oldest friend, my hero. But that shifter didn't see little me running toward him until I was right on top of him.

With a startled yelp, he fell to the ground as I threw my entire weight on top of him. A moment of triumph, and then I realized *how over my head I was.*

Effortlessly, with all the strength of a fully-grown shifter, he bucked me off. I landed with a hard thud on the ground, and before I could blink, he was on me, teeth at my neck.

And then, the next second, he was off me, laying in a motionless heap a few feet away.

I sat up, unable to help the smile that spread across my face. Maybe I was in shock. Regardless, the wolf inside howled triumphantly. We'd avenged our parents. We'd taken on two fully grown shifters and won.

I looked over at Nathan, who stood facing away from me in his human form once again, on shaky legs over the dead bodies of our foes.

But he didn't look triumphant like me. It was then that I noticed all the blood, and how he looked like he'd just crumble if the wind blew the wrong way.

I shifted. "…Nathan?"

He turned to face me, nearly unrecognizable in his injuries, and collapsed.

I squeeze my eyes shut, desperately trying to push those old, intrusive thoughts away.

"You don't get it. You think I want this? I can't help that I'm not good enough for her." My voice cracks. "I'm… not good enough."

"What the hell are you talking about? You are good enough. You're her damn mate."

I shake my head then turn around, staring down at the slowly dying fire so I don't have to stare at Nathan's face anymore. At the evidence that I wasn't good enough.

"I'm not going to fight for her, because when I fight for something, it always falls apart. She's better off without me anyway. I learned my lesson. Now let's stop talking about this or let's fight."

Nathan doesn't answer.

I glare up at him, expecting him to finally agree to a fight. Good. That's what I want. That would do more to burn some of this depression off than sitting around talking about *feelings*. My wolf could always go for a good fight. It's just the nature of a wolf shifter who grew up too fast, who was molded by violence.

But Nathan doesn't look angry. Doesn't look ready to fight. If anything, he just looks confused. And then recognition crosses his face as he finally figures out that I'm not only talking about Jess.

He reaches up, touching his scars, as if reminding himself they're still there. "Fucking hell, Troy. Stop feeling sorry for yourself, because I don't feel sorry. Every morning I wake up and I thank God that I have these, because it means I survived, and I was able to find Ellie."

It's my turn to be confused. "If I hadn't tried to jump into the fight..."

He shakes his head, cutting me off before I can finish my thought. "Then I would've died. You ignored my order to stay inside, but it was the right thing to do. I never said it before, but..." He looks me in the eye, and there's so much emotion there that I'm taken aback. Speechless. "Thank you. It was all worth it."

I blink at him, then at Blake, who is watching us intently. I had no idea Nathan felt that way. I thought it impossible for him to be so... at peace with everything. It's hard to be at peace, wondering about all the unanswered questions, like who or why our parents had to die. Why we had to endure the injustice of three orphaned wolf shifter pups being left to fend for themselves. Why one of us was permanently disfigured.

"You hate the way you look. You hate the way humans look at you," I say.

Nathan smirks at my bluntness. "Ellie helped me realize it's all okay," he finally says, shrugging. "She gives me a reason to wake up in the morning. Gives me a reason to look forward to tomorrow. She reminds me to keep looking forward instead of bitching and moaning about the past." He takes a breath, then looks at me, hard. "I can't imagine losing her. And that's why I'll never stop pushing you to fight for Jess. The alternative in unimaginable. It's no way to live."

I know he's right. But it still doesn't change the way Jess feels. "She doesn't want me," I say, a pleading edge to my voice, like I can somehow make him understand. "She doesn't want me. I've tried." I rake my heads through my hair, exasperated. "I'll never live up to her expectations for a mate. Husband. Whatever."

"She misses you too, you know!" Ellie calls from the front porch. Nathan smiles big at his mate, and I just scowl, wondering how long she's been listening. Doesn't matter, I guess. She's pack now, too. Our dirty secrets are hers now.

And the weird thing? She doesn't care. Doesn't look at us any differently. I long for that with my own mate, but I just don't see how it'll ever happen.

But... Ellie knows my mate well. If she says she misses me... "She said that?" I hate that there's a little tinge of hope in my voice. Especially since I've worked so hard to squash it.

"Well, no, but I can tell. Trust me. She'll come around with time. You just have to give her that time. She's been working toward another life for a long time, and just as it's in reach, you come in and stomp all over it."

I growl out a sound of offense, but she just puts a hand up. "I'm not saying it's a bad thing or you two aren't meant to be together. I'm just saying it's a lot to swallow. It's a big life change."

I want to argue, but Ellie is right. My heart squeezes at the memory of Jess, sitting in her parent's big, quiet, empty mansion, studying that laptop like it would give her all life's answers. And the inner turmoil on her face as she explained the application process, how much she's always wanted to go to medical school, and then how conflicted she feels.

Because of me.

Everyone has been telling me to give Jess space, to give her time. I thought I was doing just that, but now I see I wasn't doing that at all. I was giving her time compared to what my wolf wanted, but I was still moving too fast. I was still pressuring her to be my mate, when there's so many other things going on in her life that maybe that's not what she needs right now.

In time, Jess will see that we're meant to be together. After she figures out what she wants out of life. Until then, I'm going to stick beside her. If not as a mate, as a friend.

As the best damn friend she's ever had.

Ellie gives me an irritating knowing look, like she can tell her words have sunk in, but I just ignore her as I push past Nathan and Blake toward my cabin.

For the first time all week, my cabin doesn't feel oppressively lonely. There's hope once again, and though it's terrifying, I vow not to think of the worst-case scenario. Instead, I beeline for my keys on the kitchen table, then head back outside.

"Where are you going?" Nathan asks as I mount my bike.

I huff a little laugh, half in disbelief of what I'm about to do, too. It's exactly what I didn't want to be talked into doing when Nathan and Blake joined me, and yet somehow, I'm about to do it anyway.

"I'm going to find Jess."

He smiles wide at me, then claps me on the back. "Don't do anything stupid," he says jokingly.

"No promises."

Chapter 11

Jess

The empty beef jerky packages crinkle under me as I roll over in bed. It's a bizarre break up food for sure. Usually it's ice cream or chocolate, but a break up with a guy like Troy calls for something different.

I have no idea why I've been pounding so much beef jerky that it's made me sick.

Well, I do know why. Only it makes me even more miserable to think about it.

My stomach makes weird gurgling noises, and I suddenly feel like if I lay down even a second longer, I'll barf. And so for the first time in what feels like days, I venture out of my bedroom and head downstairs.

My parent's house is cold, dark, and empty. They'll be home from their vacation soon, though I doubt the house will feel any more welcoming in their presence. I don't know what's worse: being miserable alone or being miserable and forcing myself to look normal around my parents.

All I want to do is cry. If everything were normal, then I'd probably be studying right now. I'd be hard at work, doing my best to get a head start on the upcoming semester. I should be focusing on wrapping up my undergraduate career with a neat little bow so I can be as prepared for medical school as possible.

But I'm not. I'm wallowing in misery because I pushed a good man, someone who makes me happy and unconditionally accepts me, away.

I pad out into the back garden, settling by the pool. My parent's garden is immaculate in that fancy, too expensive way. It's nice, but not really my taste. At least it's better than the suffocating formality of inside.

The hedges, trimmed into unnaturally symmetrical shapes, barely sway in the cool breeze. I frown, then look to my side, toward what my mother would call her "prize rose bush". The real credit should go to the gardener, I suppose, because I don't recall ever seeing my mother trim or even water it.

If it were my yard, I'd clear out all these plants. The Queen of Hearts can have them back. I'd replace everything with native plants, wild and colorful, of varying shapes and sizes. And instead of treating everything with pesticide, I'd go natural. How nice would it be to sit outside amongst the happy, chirping birds, watching the bees and hummingbirds enjoying my hard work?

I never understood what my parents have against wildlife and nature. If you hate the outdoors so much, why invest so much in a garden?

Appearances, I decide. Like everything else when it comes to my parents, that's all that matters. Wealthy people have fancy, soulless gardens, and so my parents must have one, too.

My mind wanders, and before I can stop myself, I question if Troy would appreciate a nice garden. I let out a groan and sink deeper into the patio chair. It feels like I'll never be able to get him out of my head.

The backdoor slides open, startling me out of my thoughts. My mother pokes her head outside, apparently back from vacation.

"There you are, Jessica! We were looking all over for you. Why are you sitting outside?" Mother asks, perplexed.

I sigh. "Just needed some fresh air."

"Well come inside. Your father and I have something to show you."

She disappears into the house before I can protest, unbothered by my need for fresh air. I grumble a little under my breath, but follow her inside anyway.

Mother leads me down the hall and into Father's study, where we find him sitting behind his massive desk, looking rather pleased with himself. He slides a massive envelope toward me as I approach.

My heart drops. The words *Harvard University* scream at me in big crimson lettering. A big envelope from Harvard? It can only mean one thing.

Mother gives me an encouraging look. "What are you waiting for? Go on, open it."

With shaky hands, I open the envelope, then scan over the letter. I feel the color drain from my face as I read over the words I've imagined reading a thousand times before.

When I don't read aloud, Mother peaks over my shoulder. "You've been accepted!" She squeals, clapping her hands. "How exciting!"

I slowly nod as I stare down at the paper in my hands, unable to think of something to say. I find that I can't even fake excitement at the moment. I'm just… stunned.

"Exciting, right?" My mother repeats. "Jessica? Why aren't you saying anything?"

"Maybe she's in shock, dear," My father says.

Mother lets out a laugh. "Oh, you silly girl. You truly thought you might not get in?"

Finally, I find my voice. "I don't want to go," I blurt out.

My confession is met with silence. Mother simply blinks. For the first time since I've been born, she's speechless. Father wordlessly gets to his feet, walks to the cabinet across the room, and pours himself a glass of scotch.

Mother clears her throat. "You can't be serious."

I knew this would be hard. Even harder now than if I had said something long ago. But I hadn't sorted my feelings or made a decision until now. It's like, once I got this acceptance letter, my head finally cleared. Of course I'm not going. It's so obvious now. This is not the direction my life is supposed to go. There were so many signs that I ignored, so much unhappiness I put up with, until I met Troy.

And I have to tell my parents at some point. Better late than never, I guess.

I take a deep breath, steeling myself to explain, but my father interrupts. "Where is this nonsense coming from?" His voice is stern, reminding me of the time I was ten and I embarrassed him by throwing a tantrum in front of his country club buddies.

"I've been thinking about it for a while now," I answer. My voice comes out quieter than I want it to.

Mother lets out a dramatic wail, throwing her hands in the air, then looks at Father. "Where did we go wrong?"

Though I try to be calm and rational, her words irritate me. Neither of them will be quiet long enough for me to explain anything. They're less concerned about my happiness, more concerned about how they'll look as parents when their golden child suddenly decides to do something with her life other than attend an Ivy League.

"You didn't do anything wrong," I say, exasperated. "I just don't want to be a doctor. It's not the end of the world, guys. I'm still here, alive and healthy, and I'll figure something else out."

Father casts me a skeptical look, but I hold my head high, surprising even myself. Never did I think I'd have this moment with my parents, and I'm stunned — and proud — of myself for sticking to my guns and holding my ground.

"What do you want to do, then? Your father has

connections elsewhere, too. Yale, Dartmouth, Princeton…"

I cut her off. "No. None of those. I mean, I don't know. I don't want to do anything like that. I think I want to stick around here, closer to home." Strategically, I neglect to mention Troy. It'll have to be another time, if we even get back together. Right now, my parents are already in meltdown mode. I don't know what mode is below that, but I don't want to test it by bringing up my wolf shifter lover.

"You *must* have a plan," my father insists.

"I don't though, okay? And it'll all be fine! You don't think I'm capable of figuring something out? You haven't even given me a chance!" My calm is splintering. My voice comes out a little louder than intended, and my father's face goes red.

"Do you know how much we've done to make sure your dreams come true?"

"That's just it! This isn't my dream! It's never been my dream, you just didn't realize it. Maybe I never wanted to be a doctor. Maybe I only thought I did because it's a prestigious title and it's what has always been expected of me!" I feel myself unraveling. It's too late, though. My throat gets tight and tears prick at the corners of my eyes. So much for standing strong. "Maybe I like beef jerky more than chocolate! Or Bud Light more than wine! The point is, I was never given a choice. I don't want this," I say, vaguely motioning around me at the house, "I don't want any of it, and you never saw it because you were only willing to see your daughter as a doctor!"

I'm out of words, my brain a jumbled mess, as my parents stare at me in stunned confusion.

"What does this have to do with beef jerky?" Mother asks. I almost want to laugh, but I can't. But I can't explain myself either. The walls of my father's office feel like they're closing in, and all I want to do is escape.

I fling the envelope back onto Father's desk. "I can't do

this right now," I say, then turn on my heel and jog down the hallway, toward the front door.

Neither of them try to stop me on the way out, and I don't stop to grab any clothes or my phone charger or any of those other little things that I'll need. I leave with no plan, and though it's utterly stupid and terrifying, it feels better than staying another minute under my parent's oppressive roof. Surely they'll come around eventually. After all, I don't doubt that they love me, but we're clearly not on the same page. Not even in the same book.

And until all of us have had time to calm down, I need to get away.

The heavy front door slams behind me as I step outside, the cold night air stinging the salty wetness on my cheeks.

"Jess?"

I stop in my tracks as the voice of the one person I want to see most hits my ears. My head snaps to the end of the driveway, where Troy sits atop his motorcycle, barely illuminated by the lamp posts.

"Troy?" My voice is barely a whisper, but I know he can hear it. He climbs off his bike, all muscles and wind-blown hair. He smiles big as I jog up to him, at least until I'm close enough for him to see that my eyes are puffy and my mascara is running. His eyes go wide as I break out into a sprint, crashing into his massive chest and letting out all the emotions I've been holding back. The dam breaks wide open.

Soothingly, he rubs my back, holding me close and whispering desperate, comforting words into my hair as I blubber into his shirt.

After a few minutes, when I've managed to catch my breath, he pulls away just enough to tilt my chin up towards him. "Tell me what's wrong, Jess. Tell me so I can fix it." He pleads like my tears physically hurt him.

I swallow hard. "Do you prefer roses or wildflowers?"

He cocks his head in confusion as my words register.

"Don't lie. Don't think about it. Just say it. Roses or wildflowers."

His eyes scan my face, searching for something.

Finally, he answers. "I know I should say roses, but I think I like wildflowers better." There's a hesitance in his voice, and shyness, like he doesn't want me to disapprove but he doesn't want to lie to me, either. "Don't get me wrong, roses are pretty, but they don't touch the beauty of a field full of wildflowers."

He looks at me, uncertainty in his eyes. "Is that the wrong answer?" he asks, joking to cut the tension.

I shake my head and smile, then throw my arms around his neck, crashing my lips against his.

Chapter 12

Jess

Troy clearly has no idea what is going on as I pace in front of him. He sits on the bed of the motel room we're staying in, staring at me as I verbally think aloud, recounting my last conversation with my parents.

I can't help but think how every turning point in our relationship has started either in a motel room or with him sitting on a bed as I stand in front of him. The thought sends a shiver down my spine. Is this the part where we confess our love for each other, or is this the part where he doubles down, says I've broken his heart too many times, and tells me he doesn't want anything to do with me anymore?

With a shake of my head, I cast those thoughts out of my mind for the moment. There are more pressing concerns, like the fallout with my parents and the realization that, if my parents are mad enough, I might not have anywhere to go.

I unload everything about what happened onto him, and like a great boyfriend — erm, friend — he listens intently, nodding and frowning at appropriate times. Though I'm still upset, I feel immeasurably better just because Troy is here with me.

"I just don't know what to do next," I admit.

He pats the spot on the bed beside him and I sit down.

"You do whatever you want, Jess. What is that?"

I swallow hard at the question. My parents asked the same thing, but it was more of an accusation. I could tell there was no right answer unless it was an enthusiastic "I'm going to Harvard!"

But with Troy, it's different. I can tell he wants my honest thoughts. The problem is that I truly don't know what I want. I don't know what makes me happy.

Until now, my life has been a smooth ride as long as I've stayed on the path paved by my parents. It feels like I've suddenly jerked the wheel though, choosing to nosedive off the nearest cliff.

The uncertainty makes me want to scream out of both frustration and fear. Troy looks at me expectantly. Afraid that I might actually scream in his face if I open my mouth, I just give him a weak shrug.

He frowns at me. "You don't have to make this some big existential problem, Jess. Just think about what you enjoy doing."

He's blunt, but I actually appreciate it. There's no malice in his tone. It's just who he is. And sometimes I need that, I think. Too often I spiral in my own thoughts and end up giving control over to my parents so that I don't have to face the stress. Troy is good for me. He doesn't let me retreat when I get scared.

And so I close my eyes and think for a moment. Quietly, he sits beside me, giving me the space to think about what I truly want out of life while also being a strong, comforting presence.

"I guess I have a few ideas," I finally answer. "But it's terrifying. I'm all on my own without my parents. And I've never had to deal with that before."

Troy reaches for my hand, his features softening. "You don't ever have to be alone," he says quietly.

His hand is so warm and inviting, and I want so

desperately to crawl in his lap, but I restrain myself. I'm so grateful he was conveniently nearby when I was about to fall apart, but at the same time, I don't really know why he's here. I don't want to misinterpret anything. I don't know if either of our hearts can handle that.

The last I saw him, he broke up with me because I wasn't willing to commit. It was justified, too. And I certainly never expected him to change his mind.

I hope he has, but I don't want to assume. Since we met, there hasn't been a moment that we've been on the same page. I'm tired of that.

I squeeze his hand, then look at him. Really look at him. Am I imagining that he looks a little thinner than the last time I saw him? A little more haggard? It gives me a strange guilty pleasure to think that maybe he was as miserable as I was this whole week. His stubble is now a moderate beard, his hair a little more grown out. Even the brightness in his eyes has faded a little. And even with all those changes, he's still breathtakingly beautiful.

I can't help myself. I reach out, touching the warmth of his cheek lightly. He leans into my hand, then clasps his own over it like he doesn't want me to let go.

"Why did you come back?" I ask.

He takes a deep breath, and internally, I do the same, preparing myself mentally for him to really break my heart this time. To seal the coffin, so to speak. I'd deserve it, really.

"I can't stay away from you. I tried. I really did. I wanted to give you space. I want you to be happy, and if that means you find somebody else, then I'll have to live with that. But I couldn't let you go completely. Not without trying to be in your life somehow. If only as a friend."

His voice cracks on the last word, and though he gives me a small smile, his eyes give away his true feelings. He's willing to be my friend, though it'll hurt like hell.

"You're willing to be my friend? Only my friend?"

He swallows, then nods, looking like he's in utter agony.

And I hate it. It feels like torture for both of us, apparently.

"I've been an idiot," I whisper. "In all aspects of my life. But especially with you."

His brows shoot up at my admission, and I half want to cry, half want to laugh at his reaction. I've really done a number on this guy if he thinks I'm not at all sorry about how everything played out between us.

But he doesn't say anything. He just sits silently, a slight look of confusion on his face. Maybe he doesn't completely understand. Or maybe he doesn't know what to say because he's already moved on.

Again, we just aren't on the same page. But I'm determined to get us there. My heart pounds like a drum in my chest and I'm more nervous than I was even when I confronted my parents. I steel myself.

"I want to be with you. Completely. Not as your friend. As your mate."

He blinks at me, and then I know the moment my words sink in, because his eyes fill with hope and roughly drags me into his lap until I'm straddling him.

I wrap my arms tightly around his neck as he buries his face in my neck, breathing deeply. "Is that okay?" I giggle, as if his reaction isn't enough of an answer.

He jerks away from me, just far enough to where we can see each other, but still keeping me in his iron arms, then nods. "Is it okay? It's more than okay," He says, his voice cracking on the last word. "You're everything I've ever wanted. You wanting to be my mate? I…" he trails off then shakes his head, his Adam's apple dipping as he swallows hard. "I'm the happiest man in the world. In all the worlds."

His lips are soft and sweet against mine as he gently kisses me. It's sweet and sappy and exactly what I needed after everything I've been through — everything *we've* been through — even if I didn't realize it before.

I think I knew it all along, though. Deep down, at least. Maybe I didn't know that we were destined to be mated, but from the moment I met him, I knew there was something special between us. I knew that I felt at home in his arms.

He kisses me slowly, gently. Sweet little kisses as he tenderly cups my face in his hands. My heart feels like it'll burst from all the love and emotion I feel for the man.

He makes me feel safe and secure and believed in. He loves me, and I love him.

I still under his lips at the realization. I… love him. Troy's eyes flutter open as I let out a little gasp of surprise.

He only has a brief moment to look confused before I pull him impossibly closer, then smash my lips against his again. He lets out a hiss of pleasure and longing as I kiss him again, harder, and nip at his bottom lip. His returning kisses become more and more urgent as I run my hands over his strong shoulders, over his broad chest, then clutch at his tee shirt. I let out a little whimper, because that always-present pool of warmth I feel when I'm around Troy strokes into a blazing inferno, and suddenly, I can't stop touching him.

I thrust my chest against his, desperate for more of him. He gets the hint. In one swift motion, he pulls his shirt over his head and tosses it onto the floor. My hands go to his chest. My fingers run through the hair there, then down, lightly skating over his well-defined abs. He lets out a growl, possessive and masculine, as my fingers find the button of his jeans and I flick them open.

"I'm sorry for making you wait," I somehow manage around kisses.

"I'd wait forever," he answers. His voice is low, gravelly, but he's all sincerity. My sweet, gruff, rough-around-edges mate.

I flash him a smile as he continues. "You're worth it." His hands grip my hips, finding the hem of my shirt. I wiggle on his lap encouragingly, loving the feel of his hard length through his jeans against my center.

"I've missed you. Missed your smiles," his voice is tantalizingly husky. He kisses and licks teasingly at my jaw, then my neck. My breath quickens as I throw my head back, giving him easier access as I twine my fingers in his hair.

"Your intelligence." He nips at my collarbone as I twine my fingers in his hair, loving the way his lips move against my skin but also frustrated that he is moving so slowly.

"Your eyes," he says as his hands dip under my shirt, up my back. Without effort he unclasps my bra, then rubs up and down my ribcage, teasing the skin beneath my breasts. I let out a whimper as he gently palms me, kneading the sensitive flesh there. I open my eyes to see his gaze hard on my breasts, salivating at the sight of them even under my tee shirt.

"And my boobs?" I whisper.

He lets out a chuckle, then nods, his hands falling back to my hips, grinding me down even harder against him. "Those too. Everything."

I'm so ready for him. Ready to start my new life with him. Ready to conquer the world together.

Ready for him to bite me, to claim me for good.

"Please," I whimper.

He lowers me to the bed, and we waste no time getting the rest of our clothes off. His big body is warm, and I love the way he pushes between my legs. My throat catches as he sinks in, nuzzling against my neck like he loves to do. I wrap my legs around his waist, pulling him closer, wanting to feel as connected as possible to the man above me.

I'm stretched full as he moves, in and out, drawing pleasure out of me from deep nerves I didn't even know I had. Everything feels so good, so intense…

I'm already close. I grip his shoulders tight, waiting for the bite. Waiting for the pain as he sinks his fangs into me, solidifying our bond forever. Wanting it. Craving it.

The pleasure builds until I can't hold it back. My muscles tense as he pounds into me, harder, and yet still doesn't bite.

"I'm close. Claim me," I grit out.

He slows, looking down at me, his eyes hazy with lust as the muscles of his jaw work like he's trying his so hard not to bite me.

With a deep breath, he presses his forehead to mine, looking me right in the eye, his dick still buried deep inside me. It's the most intimate position. "Not right now," he pants.

I open my mouth to protest, but he shakes his head. "I want you to be sure. Until then, you're still mine."

I understand. It's irreversible. The bite will make me a shifter. It'll change my life in every way.

His eyes search my face, waiting on me to answer. "You're mine, too," I remind him, stroking his face to let him know I understand.

He smiles, then places one big, strong hand beside my head and one hand between my legs. His thumb teases my clit as he pulls out and pushes in again. The orgasm builds again quickly, and then I'm tumbling over the edge, vaguely aware that I'm probably screaming loud enough for people in the hallway to hear.

Troy collapses on top of me, exhausted from his own release. And as he pulls me against him, cuddling me like I'm the most precious human on Earth, my heart melts.

Troy cares about me. Out of anyone, he's the one person who has always, from the beginning, just wanted me to be happy.

And in this moment, I couldn't be happier.

Chapter 13

Jess

I already know my parents are watching as Troy pulls up the driveway on his motorcycle, me straddled to his back. My mother is probably peeking out the window, clutching her metaphorical pearls, as my father stoically pounds back an expensive scotch.

Telling them I'm not changing my mind about medical school, and oh, by the way, I'm dating a wolf shifter, is going to be a riot. That's if I can even stick up for myself. There's a small part of me that worries I'll fall back into old habits. When they press me for details or to explain myself, I'm afraid I'll bend to their will. What if I get too frazzled, just like last night, and can't keep my composure?

Troy senses my nerves as we hop off his bike and head for the front door. He slips his hand in mine and squeezes, silently telling me to remember the plan, and reminding me that he's got my back.

We reach the front door and hesitate. To knock or not to knock. I feel like a stranger in my parent's house. For a moment, Troy and I stand shoulder to shoulder, staring at the heavy double doors before us.

"You can do this," Troy says reassuringly.

I nod, take a deep breath, then push the door open.

Unsurprisingly, Mother and Father are waiting in the foyer. I am surprised, however, to see my mother looking worse for the wear. Never in my life have I seen her without perfectly groomed hair or a full face of makeup. And yet now, she stands before us, tired and pale and wearing freaking sweatpants.

I didn't even know the woman owned sweatpants.

Mother gives me a small, hopeful smile before her eyes flicker to Troy. Her eyes go wide at the sight of him.

"Mother, Father... this is Troy."

Father stares impassively at us. "Um, hello." Mother says faintly.

Clearly just as uncomfortable as the rest of us, Troy responds with a nervous wave. I've thrown the poor guy into a weird family dynamic. Even if he's come willingly, he deserves a reward later, I absently think.

An awkward silence descends upon us as we all stare at each other. No one knows what to say. It should fall on me to speak first, but there's just so much to explain. Where do I even start?

My heart starts racing, and I half consider grabbing Troy's hand and making a break for it. We can come back later, or even another day.

But Troy squeezes my hand again, reminding me that I can do this.

I take a deep breath. "Troy is a shifter," I start, then trail off. It's a stupidly obvious statement. My parents would have to be blind not to put two and two together. Troy's blazing blue eyes, bulging muscles, and unnaturally good looks are textbook shifter.

Mother and Father both nod, waiting for me to continue. I can see it in their eyes that they both want to know why I've brought this strange man into their home.

"He's my boyfriend. My... mate."

Mate. The word rolls off my tongue so naturally. It's the

first time I've announced it to someone other than Troy, and yet it feels so right.

"He's the reason you suddenly don't want to attend Harvard?" Father asks. The words were probably more biting in his head, but in the face of a hard wall of muscle like Troy, it comes out less than intimidating. With Troy around, Father is no longer the big dog, and I can tell he's out of his element.

I sigh, because I knew that's what my parents would deduce from this. "No. Not at all. What I told you last night was the truth. I don't think I ever wanted to be a doctor. Troy is just a bonus thing I needed to tell you guys about."

Father looks unconvinced, and I feel my blood start to boil in frustration. There's nothing I can say to make my parents believe me.

This is going about as well as last night, meaning it's quickly nosediving into total disaster.

Troy clears his throat from beside me. "May I say something?"

My parents look both stunned and scared at the sound of his voice, and I might've giggled if we weren't in such a tense situation. Neither of my parents have ever spent any real amount of time around shifters. Shifters and people like my parents rarely have overlapping social circles.

Troy casts me an uncertain look, and I just smile and nod encouragingly, curious about what he wants to say. "Of course you can speak," I say softly.

He clears his throat again, then addresses my parents directly. "I know how it looks. I'm nothing but a bad influence. I've found your daughter and am selfishly pulling her to the dark side," he chuckles, but my mother's eyes go wide, missing the humor.

"He's joking," I add before mother faints.

"Erm, yeah. It's a joke," Troy says quietly. "What I mean is, it's not like that at all. She's my mate, and if you know anything about shifters, you'd know that means I'd never do anything to hurt her. I only want what's best for her. I just want her to be happy."

He squeezes my hand again, more for his benefit than mine this time. "Your daughter is the smartest and strongest woman I've ever met. If she truly wanted to go to Harvard, I wouldn't stop her. But I also know I've never seen her show that she wants to be a doctor. Not even a little bit. Jess has so much passion and intelligence to share with the world. I think she should put those strengths to use in a career of her choosing, especially if that makes her happier than going to medical school."

His words warm me from the inside out, and I feel my cheeks flush with his praise.

I peel my eyes from Troy back to my parents, wondering if they'll argue with him. Wondering if they'll admit that they'd rather have a doctor daughter than a happy daughter, or if they'll feel shamed enough from Troy's speech to keep their thoughts to themselves.

Father looks silently between us, and to my surprise, Mother lets out a sniffle. Her eyes are brimmed with tears as she smiles at me. "I didn't know you didn't want to be a doctor. I guess I just wanted you to do the things I never did, and I'm only just now realizing it was wrong of me to push that on you. It seems this shifter — um, Troy — and I want the same thing. I just want you to be happy. I want you to follow your heart. From now on, I'll just stand back and cheer you on from the sidelines."

I blink at her in surprise. She hardly sounds like my mother at all, but at the same time, I believe her. It all makes sense now. Maybe she wanted to be a doctor. Maybe she wanted to be something besides a housewife. But somehow, she ended up the trophy wife to my father, and part of her regrets it.

"Thank you," I whisper, still stunned.

For a moment, it's silent as we all process what's just happened. Our family dynamic just changed in a huge way, and it'll never be the same. It's clear my parents now understand that I'm no longer willing to bend and follow all their rules just to make them happy and to keep the peace.

But that isn't a bad thing, though.

They may feel like they lost their daughter, but in reality, they never knew the real me. Now that I can be myself and voice my true thoughts, we can start the healing process.

And now that I see my mother for who she truly is, I want more than anything to heal our relationship.

I just don't know how to do it.

Mother takes a small step forward, casting a nervous glance at Troy. "W-would you two like to join us for lunch?"

I smile, but before I agree, I look to Troy questioningly. He sticks out like a sore thumb in my parent's house, and I know he's uncomfortable. But he just shrugs, then gives my mother a small, disarming smile, letting me know he'll be okay. He's willing to put up with this ridiculous, overly fancy circus for another hour or two for my sake, and I love him all the more for it.

As expected, lunch is awkwardly formal, though I find it easier than normal to muster the patience to endure it. After we finish, I watch with amusement as Troy politely pretends to enjoy a glass of scotch my father offers.

I exchange a look with my mother, and I think she actually understands. And surprisingly, I feel content.

There's hope that the future will be bright for us all. My parents will eventually come around to whatever career path I choose, even if it's not prestigious and I don't make a six-figure salary. Well, my mother will come around at least, and she can convince my father on the matter.

And though they're both still a little hesitant about Troy, anyone with eyeballs could see that he truly loves me. If their only fault with him is that he's a shifter, they'd never say it to his face. And I'm confident that, in time, they'll see the amazing man I see underneath that rough, slightly scary exterior.

I smile as Troy takes another sip of the scotch he so accurately describes as poison when we're alone. He clears his throat like he's trying not to cough and blinks several times. I pat his leg under the table, in awe of a man who's willing to drink "poison" to make me happy.

And you know what? It's working.

Epilogue

Jess

I snicker as I dump the contents of my makeup bag onto the bathroom counter and Troy looks on in horror.

"What is this for?" he asks, picking up my eyelash curler. Playfully, I rip it out of his hand, then put it up to my eye to demonstrate. His mouth falls open and it takes all I have not to bust out laughing.

"Stop that! You'll make me rip my eyelashes out!"

"Oh God, it keeps getting worse," he says.

I throw down the eyelash curler and push him out of the bathroom. Normally I love that he sticks to me like glue, but today I actually have to get ready. Today, I start my new job as general manager of the biggest — and only — garden shop in Applecross.

If someone had told me six months ago that I'd be working in a small, secluded mountain town and living in a log cabin with my wolf shifter mate, I'd have laughed in their face. But now I can't imagine life any different. I love it.

Everything has fallen into place since I moved into Troy's cabin two months ago. I get to wake up beside my mate, live next door to my best friend, and now, I get to spend my days surrounded by plants. Gardening is the one thing I've always liked, and so it was only natural that I decided to make it into a career. My parents are seemingly even on board. Though Father is still adjusting to the idea of a daughter a little less "successful" than they originally planned, Mother was over-the-moon excited when I told her about my new job at the garden center. They're even talking about coming up to visit.

I finish up my makeup (a simple look since I'll likely work up a sweat at some point today) then open the bathroom door to find Troy sitting on the master bed waiting for me. He lets out a low whistle as I walk toward him and flutter my eyelashes.

"Do I look pretty?" I jokingly ask.

He growls, pulling me down to the bed beside him. "Too pretty. You won't sell any flowers."

I look at him, confused.

"You make the flowers look bad by comparison."

I giggle at his stupid joke, then press my lips against his. Like always, I marvel at how wonderful he tastes. At the feel of his lips. The way his fingers gently graze my cheeks, pulling me in.

Somehow, I have enough willpower to push away before things get to out of hand. He lets out a very canine whine.

"I can't be late…"

"We can make it quick," he says into my neck. His teeth scrape at the sensitive skin there, teasing me and making me seriously consider calling in sick on my first freaking day.

He still hasn't bitten me, but at this point, I know it's more about the tease and build up than putting it off for any other reason. He knows how turned on I get during sex when he lightly nips at me.

And honestly? It doesn't matter much. We both know that we're mated. He's mine and I'm his. A bite doesn't change anything other than turning me into a shifter, which I'm not all that in a hurry to do.

Our make out session is interrupted by the sound of an

engine coming up the driveway. Troy's head snaps back, confused, and he sniffs the air. Before I can ask what's happening, he leaps off the bed. "Stay here," he says, his voice low. "Don't leave the house no matter what."

I open my mouth to protest but the look he casts me tells me that this is serious. Whoever is pulling up the driveway is not Grayfang, and that probably means they're trouble.

I need to leave for work *now*, but I also don't want to get mauled by a rival wolf shifter, so I nod as Troy dashes out the front door.

Curiosity takes over, though, and I make my way over to the window in the living room and peek out through the blinds. Outside, the men of the Grayfang pack stand shoulder to shoulder between the cabins and the edge of the driveway. I shiver at how fearsome they look. I've gotten so used to seeing their softer human sides that I sometimes forget that these are strong, ferocious apex predators, capable of ripping someone apart in a heartbeat.

The truck rounds the corner coming into view from the tree line, then pulls to a stop in front of the boys.

A hand touches my shoulder. I let out a little squeak of surprise as I turn to see Ellie smiling at me. "Where did you come from?" I ask, hand over my rapidly beating heart.

"Nathan told me to stay inside our cabin," she pouts. "I thought it might be more interesting if I came over here and watched through the window with you. I snuck in through the backdoor. Sorry, didn't mean to give you a heart attack."

"That's okay," I answer. Honestly, it's probably best if she's here with me anyway. I'm as useful as a noodle in a knife fight against a wolf shifter. If things do go south out there, at least Ellie can try to defend us.

"If it were shifters looking for trouble, surely they'd come in wolf form, right?" I ask as we both stare out the window.

Ellie shakes her head. "Dunno. It's definitely some Smokefurs, but I can't pick out the individual scents through the cabin and truck."

We both watch as the driver pops out of the truck. It's a man, but that's all I can tell. He faces away from us, addressing Nathan.

"Who are they?" Ellie mumbles, squinting. The man turns around.

Ellie lets out a squeal, causing all five shifters outside to look around.

"You know him?" I ask, but Ellie is already out the front door, running across the yard toward the man. Hesitantly, I follow, stepping out on the porch to get a better view of the apparently not-life-threatening situation outside.

I have an idea of who the mysterious man is based on Ellie's reaction. The only Smokefur that might possibly be allowed on Grayfang territory without a fight is Alex, the old Smokefur alpha. He's the one who saved Nathan and Ellie when they were attacked by another Smokefur last winter.

But a woman still sits quietly in the truck, making no move to get out, and I haven't a clue of who she is.

Nathan gives Alex a smile and shakes his hand before Ellie pulls him into a hug. Alex turns, greeting Troy and Blake politely. Their reception to him is less warm than Nathan and Ellie's. Blake is silent, but that's to be expected. He rarely says anything at all. But Troy? He lets out a surly grunt and narrows his eyes at Alex.

I'm simultaneously filled with adoration and annoyance for the man. He's the sweetest guy with me, alone, behind closed doors. But when other people are involved? He still has that hard edge to him. That rude and gruff exterior. He'll probably always be like that, I think fondly.

My big, rude, wolf shifter mate.

"Nathan, I need to cash in that favor now."

"Of course!" Ellie answers without missing a beat. Troy and Blake look at her like she's grown a second head, and Nathan shifts uncomfortably.

"Well… it depends on the favor," Nathan finally answers.

Ellie casts him a severe look. "He saved our lives."

Nathan takes one look at Ellie. I recognize that look, because Troy looks at me the same way. It's the look of a man who knows he probably won't say no to his mate.

"What is it?" Nathan asks, turning to Alex.

"More like… who."

At that, the woman climbs out of the truck. She's short, slight of build, and carries herself as if she wishes she were invisible. When she looks up through her thick bangs, I see her striking blue eyes are surrounded by black. Bruises dot her cheekbones and her bottom lip looks painfully swollen.

I bite back my shudder. Shifters are supposed to heal better and faster than humans. How bad must she have been injured for her to bruise like that?

Blake lets out a choked sound. Troy raises his eyebrows, then claps Blake on the back.

Alex motions for the woman to approach. Less like a wolf and more like a mouse, she nervously scurries closer.

"This is my niece, Karina, and…"

Before he can finish his sentence, she straightens her shoulders, lifts her chin, and takes a deep breath. "And I'm looking for a mate."

Thank you for purchasing and reading this book!

If you enjoyed it, please consider leaving a review on Amazon, Goodreads, or any other website of your choosing. It helps not only the author, but also your fellow readers.

All feedback is appreciated. Reviews make a huge difference.

Want More?

If you're interested in:
1. New release announcements
2. Exclusive sneak peaks
3. Giveaways
4. Learning more about the author

Then follow Mattie Waters at:
facebook.com/authormattiewaters

Printed in Great Britain
by Amazon

22285483R00057